SEX and THE SWAMI

SEX and THE SWAMI

Saurav Mishra

PARTRIDGE
A Penguin Company

ISBN:	Hardcover	978-1-4828-0073-9
	Softcover	978-1-4828-0074-6
	Ebook	978-1-4828-0072-2

Partridge books may be ordered through booksellers or by contacting:

Partridge India
Penguin Books India Pvt.Ltd
11, Community Centre, Panchsheel Park, New Delhi 110017
India
www.partridgepublishing.com
Phone: 000.800.10062.62

CONTENTS

May the merciful Lord look upon his children with mercy and forgiveness for our acts in ignorance.

Let us pray to the Almighty Lord to guide us in our moments of sorrow and forget him not in our moments of joy.

May the Almighty Lord show us the path that brings us closer to the truth of life.

May the Lord show kindness and shine brightly within all our hearts.

Om! Peace! Peace! Peace!

CHAPTER ONE

ENCOUNTER WITH DEATH

As I slowly opened my eyes I found myself lying in front of the beach. The scene was so exotic I find it hard to explain. The weather was cloudy and the breeze of the ocean, cool and pleasant. Surprisingly, I was the only one there. For a moment I wondered whether I was in a dream. Never mind if I was, it was so beautiful that I wanted to enjoy every moment of it. In few moments from then I heard a voice calling out to me.

"Mr. Nikhil, enjoying the view?"

"Yes, it's magical," I replied, wondering who it was I was speaking to.

As I turned around I saw this gentleman, perhaps in his mid-30s, fair-complexioned, light blue eyes, about 6 feet 2 inches, staring at me, with a very warm affectionate look.

"Do I know you?" I found myself asking him.

"Perhaps not, Sir. I am the chauffeur from your hotel."

"Hotel? What hotel?" I thought.

Just then all the memories came back after being so enchanted by the beauty of the beach.

I was on holiday with my wife and children and my business associates in Malaysia.

I had come to the beach in the morning since my wife was busy making arrangements for an evening party we were hosting for our new business partners in Malaysia. And yes, I had requested for a chauffeur to pick me up at 11 a.m. But somehow it seemed a lot later . . . perhaps I had dozed off.

"What time is it?" I asked the chauffeur.

"Sir, 11 a.m., just as you requested."

"Well, I guess the clouds must be making it look so," I thought.

Nonetheless I found it a little strange that I was the only one on the beach, and it was looking so much more beautiful than I could ever recollect.

We walked a while, and there I saw this limousine standing in all its splendor waiting to drive me back to the hotel.

Well, I did consider myself a successful industrialist.

Hailing from a humble background from India I had climbed the ladder of success to head a company with a turnover of over 100 million US dollars.

As I got into the limousine I poured myself a glass of wine and started thinking about my journey in life. I remembered how with great difficulty I convinced my father to let me go to Delhi to pursue my education. My first job, how I starved for days because I had no money. When I met my wife, Meher, who showed so much confidence in me. My parents who were always there to support me. The birth of my first child and then my second and then my third. Oh, what a beautiful bunch of rascals they are, I thought. Today at 50 years of age, I believed God had granted me a good life. Well, there were downsides, but I guess they were the lessons that made me what I was today.

I don't remember when I dozed off, but when I woke up I saw my chauffeur sitting across me.

"Whoa!" I cried out. "What are you doing here, and who's driving the car?"

"Don't worry sir, the other chauffer is," he calmly replied.

"What bloody audacity? How dare you sit here sipping on my wine! Stop the car and get out!"

"I'm afraid I cant do that, Sir."?

"Like hell, not! Driver, stop the car!" I shouted.

My first reaction was that I was being kidnapped.

"Relax, Mr. Nikhil. I guess it's time to introduce myself."

I tried to be calm and managed to tell him, "Look mister, whoever you are, you are not going to get a penny from me."

I could hear him chuckle at my words.

"My name, Sir, is Yama, the lord of death."

"Yes, yes," I mumbled. "Which organization are you from, and what do you want?" I managed to ask.

He chuckled again, and said, "I am in the business of death and, I am here to give you company till your next journey that starts in six months Earth time from now."

I couldn't help but laugh out loud. "What's this, some kind of a dumb TV show with hidden cameras? Stop the goddamn car," I screamed again.

"It's been two days since you have been dead, Mr. Nikhil and, your cremation will be starting in another hour," his now powerful voice echoed into my ears.

Just then I felt my hands being gripped and I felt as if I was fainting.

I seemed to have gone into a different dimension, a different time zone.

I found myself in a house with many people, many of whom I recognized but could not really place. The house looked familiar—I vaguely recollected that it was my house in Mumbai. I saw a lady sitting in a corner arranging things but looking very sad. I knew her. Yes, of course, she was Meher, my wife. I saw my children, my parents, my sisters and relatives. All were there, but somehow I was feeling very distant from them, as if they were someone I knew from long before. I saw a body being carried away. I strongly felt that I must follow it.

It was mine, but here I was, I said to myself.

The body was set on fire. I did not feel the burning. It was as if they were burning some puppet of mine.

As the body burnt, all my memories started fading away. I stared to forget about my wife, my family and even wondered if I ever had one. Everything was like a vague distant dream slowly fading away as the fire blazed with all its glory.

CHAPTER TWO

THE TRUTH OF LIFE

I suddenly found myself awake, sitting in the limousine staring at the face of death with my life as a vague distant dream, emotionless about anything that ever happened in that life.

Only, this moment felt real.

Here I was, conscious about my current being, the past just a dream.

"That was not my death—I had just gone off to sleep and had a dream," I found myself telling Yama, still feeling disoriented about where I was, who I was and what was happening.

"And so this too will be like a dream, Mr. Nikhil, till you wake up to find yourself in another dream," the carrier of death replied.

As I came to terms with what was happening, accepting the situation as it slowly sank in, not really sure of what was happening, I asked, "Sir, if you are the lord of death, tell me then, am I dead now or am I alive, since the so-called death seems like a dream and, this moment real?"

Yama smiled at me and replied, "Do you wish to know?"

"Might as well," I said, still doubting the credentials of a man who called himself the lord of death.

"And so I shall," he said. "Can you call a dream real, Nikhil?"

"Of course not . . . even a child can tell you that," I replied disdainfully.

"When you awake from a dream do you lament and cry for the loss of the dream?"

"You claim to be the lord of death and here you are asking me silly questions. Which stupid person cries over a dream? Of course not."

"If not, then understand that there is no such thing as death: what you call death is a shift from one thought to another, from one dream state to another. Neither do you exist, neither do I, neither do the gods. If one is never born, how can one ever die just like in a dream?"

"I don't know about that, but I do know that I am dreaming right now," I replied, "and whatever is happening will be over, and soon I will wake up."

"Yes, of course you will, Mr. Nikhil, just to another dream state. We are all a reflection of thought that is being exhibited by the Creator who is now in a dream state.

"In the dream state that the Creator is in now He has created this world that we belong to, giving it a form different from His other aspect which is formless.

"The Creator in His dream state has created everything that is there, and also Man, who is a direct reflection of the Creator Himself. He alone is the enjoyer of all His creation and we are the tools through which he enjoys."

"But then why is there suffering?" I asked defiantly, wanting to get into a debate with him. "Does the Creator also suffer?"

I heard the same chuckle as when children ask simple questions.

"Many ignorant souls question the very existence of the Creator—as you do—and debate foolishly saying that if there was God then why does suffering exist.

"To that I will say that for the Creator there is neither pleasure nor suffering. Pleasure and pain are defined by Man, who lives his life not knowing its true nature.

"For the Creator, they are just a variety of different thoughts, both His creation, His consciousness, His bliss, but not His suffering.

"How can the Creator suffer, Mr. Nikhil? He is the creation of all that is. But let me explain.

"In a dream you get shot from a gun. Who suffers? You? Or that reflection in your dream who mistakes himself to be the real you? *It is the reflection who suffers.* Because he mistakes himself to be the real you and, not a reflection of your thought in a dream state.

"Similarly, Nikhil, the Creator does not suffer, but we do, because we mistake our identity to be real and not a dream of the Creator. The moment we realize this, our suffering too shall disappear.

"By the grace of the Creator there is in all of us the Creator's spark and, it is waiting to be discovered. This is the free will that the Creator has gifted us with. Live a life of ignorance—or one with total consciousness and bliss. Be warned that this choice belongs to every individual, and no one, not even Lord Vishnu can grant us that boon."

"Lord Vishnu, the preserver of life," I thought. "Do they really exist? I mean, the concept of Brahma, Vishnu and Shiv?" I asked as if I had begun to enjoy the discussion.

"The Holy Trinity as you understand is very different from what it really is," continued Yama. When the Lord created the three worlds it was a creation of thought. Therefore, everything that exists is thought particles and not really solid, liquid or gas particles as we perceive.

"Let me cite an example. When we dream, we see people, houses, mansions, oceans, etc., etc. Now spend some time pondering over your dream. Are the objects that we perceive really in a solid, liquid or gas form? No, it is in thought, created from thought particles.

"Similar is the creation of the three worlds. *Bhur*, *Bhuva*, *Swaha* (the physical, the astral, and the casual).

"The Creator's first manifestation was Lord Vishnu. Having all the attributes of the Creator, one may say Vishnu is the creator of all that is.

"It was from Vishnu that Brahma was created wherein Brahma thought he was the Creator and not Vishnu, thus giving the first instance of the birth of ignorance and false ego.

"Carefully introspect that as thought particles of God and the gift of His spark within us and the grace of intellect we have all the attributes of the Creator. However, somewhere we got attracted to the artificial creation and mistook the unreal to be the real.

"Through Vishnu, Brahma was created and, through Brahma the casual bodies were created. These casual bodies were and are extremely enlightened souls and incredibly subtle in nature.

"However, with the birth of ignorance and false ego also in the casual world routed through Brahma, the law of karma got activated."

Interrupting Yama, I asked, "Why then could the Creator or Lord Vishnu not intervene and stop the damage?" as if asking accountability from the board of directors.

With a smile Yama replied, "Free will. Remember what God gifted us with: it's your choice to do as you please because you are me, and I can choose whatever it is that I want.

"With ignorance," continued Yama, "Karma automatically comes into play."

"What is this karma?" I asked, "And why does it affect us?"

"The first thing you must understand here is that karma is not punishment but, the reaction to an action when done in a state of ignorance. The Creator in His manifested state has three basic aspects, that is one extreme, the middle, and the other extreme. Neither extreme can be defined as good or bad. When we act in ignorance this aspect of the Creator gets activated in a controlled manner, granting you all the three aspects that are related to your action or desire, thus resulting in action having a reaction, working like a see-saw.

"Because one acts in ignorance he suffers, defining it as good or bad. As I told you before, Nikhil, for the Creator they are just a variety of different thoughts, both His creation, His consciousness, His bliss, but not His suffering.

"Once the souls of the casual world came under the purview of karma, lower worlds were created, thus giving birth to the astral world.

"There are countless astral worlds, from the lowest to highest and, depending on one's karma a suitable life is chosen for the person either coming from the casual world, astral world or from the physical world.

"You, Mr. Nikhil, are currently in the astral world. Depending on one's karma one either keeps going up or going further down. There are astral worlds where beauty knows no bounds, and there are astral worlds where there is darkness and evil."

"So, what happens to me? Am I going up or going down?" I asked as if waiting for my test results with an attitude that reflected as if I didn't care.

With an affectionate smile Yama held my hand and I found myself in the most beautiful and exotic place my eyes had ever set upon. It was like poetry: the skies, the stars, the galaxies. I could not hold back the tears as I fell on my knees and could visualize the entire existence of the universe as would the Creator. It was a moment that cannot be described with the limitations of words. It was an experience that could somewhat loftily be defined as *bliss*. No, perhaps not even that. No words were suitable for this moment. "Oh God, don't let this moment ever stop," I mumbled to myself, "this is what the Creator wants us to see, feel and enjoy." I now realized that I was truly in the company of Yama the lord of death and cursed myself for doubting the Lord Himself.

Falling at his feet I begged for forgiveness.

Yama held me up and asked, "Now do you see?"

"Yes, my lord," I replied realizing for the first time in whose company I was.

"It is your karma that you have been blessed for this moment, but you still have to overcome your karma on Earth for which you will have to go back after this moment of rest, in six months Earth time.

"Your soul will be refreshed, as you will be born again and free will, will be your gift. Your experience here will help you and guide you; there will be moments when you will feel the truth and then in those moments it will be your choice to accept or find the thought foolish and go on with your life in the endless cycle of birth and death as you understand it."

If that was the case, I thought, let me understand more, hoping this knowledge would make me be born with a stronger resolution of understanding the truth.

"Tell me, O lord, do all people after death meet you and partake in the experience that I am having?"

With a hearty laugh the lord said, "Oh, have mercy on me. Thousands of deaths take place in the physical and astral worlds every day. I would be too overstressed," he said, making me realize even the lord of death had a sense of humor.

"No, Nikhil," he replied, "it is your karma that has made you deserve this journey. After death most people go into a deep state of rest in the astral world and are again manifested on the physical plane. Some highly evolved souls go to high astral planets and rarely but surely some achieve freedom from the bondage of all the three planes and merge with the supreme consciousness and become one with Vishnu. This is what Krishna, the avatar of Vishnu, tried to explain. On the physical plane one can be one with Vishnu and enjoy the beauty of creation just as he did.

"But then there is so much darkness and ignorance in the physical plane that it is difficult for mankind to overcome this veil of ignorance—but it is not impossible.

"It was on further degradation and ignorance of the soul on the astral plane that the physical plane got manifested.

"Understand that heaven and hell are not defined by good and evil, but rather by the evolution of the soul's consciousness or its ignorance."

"But then, in that case," I asked, "how can Man be made to realize this? There are—and I can say many—good souls who are seeking what you are preaching: where do they go, who will guide them, who will be there to remind them that free will exists?"

"Over the centuries many avatars are manifested in the physical plane to do just that. But the ignorance is so deep-rooted that it will take thousands of years for the physical world to reform. But eventually it will. Like I said life is a see-saw. There will be a time when the physical world will have its Golden Age (*Satya Yuga*). In this age the peoples' minds will be in tune with the Creator, then slowly ego will creep into the souls making men think of themselves as individuals and different from the Creator, thus giving rise to the Silver Age (*Treta Yuga*), followed by the Bronze Age (*Dwapara Yuga*), and finally the Iron Age (*Kali Yuga*), the age of total darkness.

"At the end of each cycle there is absolute and total destruction of all that has been in the universe (all the three worlds). This cycle of creation and destruction and creation again is a continuous process, just as we sleep, dream and awaken in a continuous process.

"Each cycle has millions of human years after which it is destroyed. After destruction Brahma is in a formless state for an equal number of years which are counted as one day and one night of Brahma.

This gets repeated for 100 Brahma years followed by the death of Brahma. There is silence for another 100 Brahma years after which there is birth of the new Brahma.

"This cycle is ever continuous by the Creator.

"Over here one must try to understand the difference between Brahma and the Creator.

"Brahma was the cause of the three worlds. But the Creator was that who was the cause of Brahma. Further to this also understand that the Creator has two aspects: one, which is the Formless, and the other with form (Vishnu) through whom Brahma was manifested.

"Today on the physical plane mankind is in the Iron Age (*Kali Yuga*) and, therefore, extremely difficult for them to realize this truth. Mankind today has lost direction due to which there is so much suffering."

"Tell me then, my lord, how in this age of Kali can Man realize this?"

"I shall tell you," replied Yama as if wanting to give everything to a child as a father would want to.

"But remember," he said with a word of warning, "it has to be *your* discovery, *your* journey.

"Now listen to what I have to say carefully," Yama spoke with affection. When Man is born on the physical plane and takes his first breath, his karma comes into action. With each breath that he inhales and exhales he does so in reverse to the nature of the Creator, slowly making him forget his true nature and identifying himself with the body and not its original form.

"Many children remember their past lives or their lives in the astral plane when born, but with the continuous process of inhaling and exhaling they slowly forget their past and start identifying themselves with their new body of flesh and blood and their current environment.

"As this physical body grows, it starts craving for things that satisfy its false ego as it feels it is he who is the doer and he the enjoyer.

"This is the first and foremost fundamental mistake a man makes. Remember, till such time one is not on the same frequency as the Creator, the law of karma is in motion and as I said, karma is like a see-saw. The moment there is a desire, there is bound to be disappointment. And so a synopsis of the life of Man on Earth is a series of desires and disappointments.

"These desires give birth to evil as Man can go to any extent to achieve what he wants thereby creating more commotion in the already complex environment.

"Look at the life of Man; look at his suffering; look at the pain in his heart due to unfulfilled desires; look how he suffers at the loss of loved ones; see the warfare, the murders the politics of power and all this for what? So that one day he may be old and become a liability for his own family and live on thoughts (like a distant dream) of what he had achieved, and eventually die with perhaps a vengeance and bitterness in his heart asking himself at last, "What was the purpose of life?"

"There are so many people who were powerful but as age caught up with them they became a liability to their own families. This is happening all the time and everywhere. Yet Man believes it will never happen to him. Who is young today will be old tomorrow, who is alive today will be dead tomorrow, yet they continue this life with such utter disregard to this reality that it is truly painful and pitiful.

"Let me share an incident with you. Once on a visit to Earth, I was standing outside a shop sipping a nice chilled cola when suddenly I heard the laughter of a young boy of 12 years. He was enjoying himself by throwing stones at a poor old man who was so weak that he could not even scream for help.

"What I found amusing was that this very old man was once upon a time a very powerful police officer who was known for his terror not amongst criminals but amongst honest people. Soon, his retirement came, but having amassed a sufficient amount of wealth, he led a comfortable life with his wife and children after retirement. His children got married and soon he became a grandfather. As time passed by his wife died, and he kept growing older. His sons and daughters-in-law started finding him a nuisance since he was always suffering from some ailment and was always complaining. Soon, his grandchildren started complaining because he was always coughing, which disturbed them in their studies. There came a time when he lost his speech and could not even walk properly due to old age. He had now gone to the extent of being a source of embarrassment for his own family. Finally his family could take no more of his nuisance and abandoned him here to live the life of a beggar."

"That's sad," I thought, and interrupting Yama, I said, "but this would not happen to *me*, would it? And neither would I let it to happen to my parents," I asserted with conviction, "that I am sure of."

"Of course, it would not happen to you: you are dead," he said, laughing as if I had said something funny.

To that, I agreed. However, I continued, "My lord, what would be my state had I lived to be old?"

"Do you wish to know?" he asked. "Yes, my lord, I do. I mean, it doesn't make a difference anymore but just for the sake of it," I said.

Suddenly, he gripped my hands and I felt faint.

As I woke up, all the thoughts had disappeared, I was alone in a room lying on a bed with a nurse sitting in the far corner. I started coughing and the nurse came running to me, asking me if I wanted anything.

"No, no, get out," I replied bitterly. As she walked away I could hear her curse me. I felt like getting up and beating her to a pulp, but I knew my paralysis of the left side and waist down would not allow me to do that. It was 12 years back, on my 70th birthday that I was struck with this attack, and ever since I was confined to this room with the routine evening and morning outings on my wheelchair. My wife Meher, oh! how much I missed her. It was 10 years since she had died and that emptiness in my heart could never be replaced. There was not a day when I never cried thinking about her. She had managed the business well, and now what has become of the empire that I built.

My sons, all three of them, were just too stupid to handle the business and now it was in a shambles.

My partners knew this and I knew how they brainwashed them into making foolish decisions and managed to take over the control of the empire by making them mere puppets.

How could I blame them? It was a jungle out there, and only the toughest and the strongest could survive. It was a world meant for lions, I knew, because I used to be one, I thought with a sigh.

I also knew deep inside that my children were waiting for me to die so that they could split the property and move their own ways with their pompous wives and spoilt, rotten children.

I think it was almost four years since any of them had visited me. Of course, I did receive their calls once in a while, but that too as a conversation that didn't last more than a minute. They spent more time talking to the nurse, especially Arjun my eldest son and she was always giggling and laughing when she was talking to him. I wonder, I thought, considering he calls me the most, talking more to her than to me.

Aah, what a life. From where I started and where it has ended. I wondered if I should change my will. I wanted to do it a long time ago but for the sake of Meher I never did. I would rather give my money to a charitable trust than to my own dirty, rotten sons.

That's a good idea, I thought, as least they will realize what is my worth. I called my lawyer and entrusted him to make a new will wherein on my death my entire assets be transferred to a variety of charitable trusts.

Now that it was done I was waiting for a family reunion since I advised my lawyer to inform them if they called him. I was sure the nurse would do the remaining needful.

It was hardly a week when around noon I heard some flutter and activity in the driveway.

"Aah," I thought, "it's reunion time." The hungry jackals had arrived and it was time to show them I still had what it took to be the lion of the jungle.

As the door to my room opened all my three sons with their wives stood there looking down on me like vultures.

"What is this, Papa?" Arjun, my eldest son spoke.

"What is what, Arjun?" I replied with defiance but feeling slightly nervous with their overpowering presence.

"You have changed your will, Papa," Akshay, my youngest son replied.

"And so I have," I said.

"What? What did you say, Papa? Speak properly!" Akshay shouted into my ear, twisting it with his powerful hands.

Tears came into my eyes, a bit because of the pain, a bit because of fear and more so because of sadness. I knew my paralysis had slightly impaired my speech but it was not as if I could not speak. And of all my sons, Akshay, the child who was the dearest to me, speaking like this.

Just then a few people entered, my lawyer who was now like a son to me, accompanied by some police officers.

"What now, Kumar?" I asked my lawyer, "am I going to be arrested for changing my will?"

Kumar came close to me, and whispered into my ears, "They are here for your protection, and please don't ask me to get rid of them. Your sons are like wounded animals right now, and capable of anything." Maybe what Kumar said was right; at least I'll be safe. "I rushed here the moment I got news that they had arrived," Kumar spoke affectionately.

"OK, Kumar, do what you feel is best," I said, perhaps with a sigh of relief.

"Gentlemen," Kumar spoke to my children, "I am afraid you'll will have to leave your father alone now, unless you wish to be arrested, and further, should you want to meet him please ensure it is done in my presence."

While leaving, Varun, my middle son shouted, "You old b******, you are nothing but a madman. Wait till you hear from us; this is not the end of it."

After they left Kumar came and sat next to me, holding my hand and trying to console me as I was still trembling from what had just happened.

"Nikhil," he spoke into my ear, "this is not going to get any easier. I have posted an officer outside the house, and the reason I came rushing is because I got a notice."

"What notice?" I asked, feeling a bit amused.

"Your children have challenged your will."

"On what basis?" I asked.

"Insanity," Kumar replied with a drawn face.

"Oh God," I thought, "Please, anything but this."

"What are my chances?" I asked.

"Well, if you haven't noticed, the nurse has gone. She is going to testify against you, and so are your associates. I have made arrangements for a replacement nurse. She should be here any moment. I don't want to give any false ideas, Nikhil, but it's going to be a messy show. And if you haven't noticed the crowd, to make matters worse the media has got a whiff of it."

My heart ached with sadness, and I asked Kumar to let me be alone.

The next morning as I woke up the new nurse came to my bedside with some tea and the newspaper as was the routine since the past I don't know how many years. As I opened the newspaper the headlines hit me like a hammer. In capital letters it read out," BUSINESS TYCOON MR. NIKHIL KR DECLARED INSANE BY FAMILY MEMBERS".

I felt faint as if I was sinking, and then all of a sudden I heard myself screaming out. "Whoa," I shouted as if I had just seen a ghost.

I was back in the limousine with Yama the lord of death sitting opposite me with a smile on his face.

"Wow, what happened just now?" I asked, still trying to recover.

"Well, you just died for the second time. You wanted to see what would happen to you till you got old, didn't you?" Yama answered.

"Yes, yes, I did. Thank God it's over.

"OK, agreed I was spared the plight," I replied, "but still I could never do that to my father."

"Of course, you wouldn't, Mr. Nikhil. You are a good soul: that's why you are here with me now and for many other reasons."

"Then please continue, my lord, as to how Man can overcome his ignorance in this age of darkness."

And so Yama continued. "As *Kali Yuga* is advancing people are moving toward the next stage, the Bronze Age (*Dwapara Yuga*)."

"But, my lord, is it not true that at the end of *Kali Yuga* the world will come to an end?"

"The world, Nikhil, comes to an end at two stages: the first in total darkness (at the end of the Iron Age, *Kali Yuga*); and the second when everyone is totally enlightened (at the end of the Golden Age, *Satya Yuga*). These cycles work in reverse order, that is from up to down and then down to up. We are currently moving from down to up, which means the current destruction will happen only at the end of *Satya Yuga*.

"Today man is so involved in his day-to-day life," continued Yama, "that he soon gets tired. He becomes like a child who is enjoying playing in the garden so much that he has forgotten about his parents and his house. As the child gets tired he suddenly realizes that he wants to go back to the warmth of his house and his parents, but has forgotten the directions to go back home.

"It is extremely important to understand, Nikhil, that it is most important for Man to have at least reached this stage if he wants to progress on this path.

"Anyone who has not reached this stage, will have to wait till his karma allows him to question himself: *'Who am I? What is the purpose of life? For what was I born? Where can I find peace?'"*

"But then, my lord," I said, "when a man reaches this stage, why do these people want to give up everything and escape?"

On hearing these words Yama replied, "Surely the Creator wouldn't want his creation to wander off into the forest. That is the reason why Krishna, an avatar of Vishnu, was born: to show mankind the way."

"Did Krishna who was as spiritual as spirituality run away into the forest, or live a life of a mendicant?"

"No, he was a truly enlightened soul who knew he was a reflection of God and, therefore, enjoyed this life as the Creator would. Once a person realizes this difference he will enjoy the beauty of all that is because then there will be no difference between him and the Creator.

"Many people in the physical plane have reached this stage where they have started asking themselves these thought-provoking questions. That's the good part. The sad part is that there many more who are taking advantage of this situation with the promise of enlightenment which, of course, has a price.

"The poor souls have reached such a stage of desperation that they are willing to pay any price for it.

"Oh, Nikhil, what price would a child not give to find directions back to his home, to the warmth of his mother? But do they actually find their way back? Unfortunately they are just driven further away always with the promise that we are almost there."

"But my lord, there must be some teachers who are genuine?" I asked.

"Of course there are, but they are rare. Understand one thing. As a disciple if you are desperately seeking a teacher, then rest assured there is a teacher even more desperately seeking you. When the time is right it is the guru who seeks out the disciple and not the other way around. And also understand the guru need not be in the physical form. He could be from a high astral planet: you just need to tune in because he has already tuned into you. Otherwise you would have not asked the thought-provoking questions in the first place.

"But of course, people are desperate. They want things fast, they want them *now*, and unfortunately that is not possible. We are not talking about buying a baseball bat, are we? But they say, 'I got the money: can you offer me peace?'

"'Sure thing,' says the vulture in saffron, 'I can offer you peace and the power of the gods, but as a man of God I do not accept money, but, of course, you may give me *dakshina*. I don't need money, but you see, money is important to run the huge infrastructure that we have (not to forget the cost of my private aircraft and a range of luxury cars, he thinks).'

"'Of course, my lord, how much do I give?' says the poor soul. 'My dear child,' replies the vulture, 'what price is enough to find God? Give up all your materialistic attachments and come into my arms. Embrace me, my child, for you are chosen by God.'

"But the competition is growing amongst the vultures, so now there are discounts being offered to people to discover God. Once on Earth I saw a poster, which said, 'Raise the kundalini and discover the unlimited untapped powers within you.' Finding the ad humorous, I decided to pay the gentleman a visit. As I entered his bungalow, I was greeted by an English lady in a sari. The ambience indeed was quite beautiful. There was greenery all around, flowers and the aroma of incense burning. The lady ushered me in and said the swamiji would meet me in a while. In the meantime I was given out a form to fill which I duly did and handed back to her. There were a lot of foreigners.

"In a while I was ushered into a large hall where swamiji greeted me and asked me to have a seat.

"'Tell me, my son, how can this man of God be of any service to you?'

"I humbly told him, 'My lord, I am in search of the truth. I feel this life is not worthy anymore and I wish to seek a higher purpose for my existence.'

"'Aah,' he exclaimed, 'then God has guided you to the right place. Tell me more about yourself,' and so I did and finally asked him how he could help me.

"'I shall make you discover the lord himself. I shall give you so much power that you will be able to achieve anything you want. But there will be a lot of hard work, and if you are ready to do that I shall give you what you could never have dreamt of,' he went on blah, blah, blah in his sweet sing-song tone.

"Now, Nikhil, let me tell you about this swami. His name was Ajay and he was born into a rich family, had a good education and was quite flamboyant in his youth as any son of a rich man would be.

"Soon, his father lost all his money, went into debt and finally died of a heart attack. This swami, being left penniless, tried his hand at all sorts of businesses but failed. Living a life of luxury he found it too humiliating to work under someone. His friends now started avoiding him, and he almost went into depression.

Being well educated he definitely knew how to play with words. One day he saw an ad that spoke about the healing powers of Reiki. He enrolled himself and after a few months got a certificate of being a Reiki Master. As a Reiki teacher he started targeting the high society clients to whom he started giving this course. They were easily vulnerable, especially the ladies as they thought it to be a noble thing to learn and teach. Soon, he started doing all sorts of courses and targeted the West, for two reasons. One, in the West life is extremely fast and such men offer them a reason to escape the highly stressful lives and, of course, the second was the money. They had an abundance of it.

"He did a lot of research on Hindu philosophy and had mastered it in words but unfortunately not in deed. His soul was evil. He enjoyed the power, the money, the respect and even the occasional sex with some of his disciples who would do anything to please him. Of course, to them he spoke not of sex but the holy science of tantra. Mind you, there was a special price for that course.

"Anyhow, there are many people like him today offering such courses, and the poor souls are easily attracted in the hope of finding peace or power."

"So, what happens now?" I asked and continued by telling him how I vaguely remembered doing such a course myself. It was quite good, I told him, remembering how refreshed I had felt after a one-week getaway. I think it was somewhere in the Himalayas.

"Of course it is good: there is no harm in such a course; it acts as a good getaway from the hectic life mankind lives, but only to get back to it again. You still get old, Nikhil, and you still continue to suffer.

"These kinds of courses are like a couple of drinks in the evening that relax you from your hectic schedule, only to get back to it again.

"If you just want to get refreshed please go ahead and join these courses; some of them I can say are even good," said Yama, "but let the ignorant men get their priorities right. Are these people looking for temporary refreshment or are they seeking a more permanent solution? If you are seeking the purpose on a permanent platform, then I am afraid to disappoint you by telling you that in the last 1,000 years the number of enlightened souls can be counted on your fingertips.

"That is the reality, Nikhil. Also, let mankind realize that to attend these courses you are in a mode of desiring to achieve something and so be warned about the see-saw. Desire results in disappointment."

"In that case, my lord, please tell me, is one who is seeking enlightenment also not a desire, to be wanting to be one with God also not a desire? Wanting to seek bliss also not a desire? And if these are all desires then there will be disappointment. Then how can Man ever be one with God—for that too is a desire?"

"Yes, Nikhil, you have spoken well, that final secret I shall tell you soon.

"But before that you must understand all the mysteries of the universe and the psychology of Man on the path of realization."

"Then please continue, my lord," I said with a sense of excitement.

"Amongst men today, there are many such vultures who are offering various remedies to Man's problems. You have a marriage problem: it can be solved; you have a money problem: it can be solved; you want your business to be successful: it can be done; you want to find God: He can be found; just call so-and-so number, and the poor foolish man spends his hard-earned money giving it to them. Just think for a moment, Nikhil, if everything was so simple would life be as it is on Earth today?"

True, I thought: it really sounds quite amusing.

"No matter how hard you try to explain to them it will be in vain, such is the age of Kali."

"Does that mean that all this astrology and all is bogus?" I asked.

"No," said Yama, "astrology definitely exists: it is a science relevant for those under the law of karma, but understand it is also not to be destined. Remember, there exists *Free Will*, but also remember this free will is relevant only once you realize that you and the Creator are one and the same."

Ignorantly, I spoke, telling Yama, "OK, so now that I know and realize this, does this now make me not subject to karma?"

Yama laughed heartily, "My dear Nikhil, free will is not like a switch that you just put it on. There are many people who talk about free will in your world. They will tell you how you can achieve anything you want, overcome anything you want, but that is not to happen till the link with the Supreme is established. Till then all the struggle and all the achievements, all the discoveries will be and are predetermined.

However, to some extent certain hurdles can be overcome by certain very advanced yogis (though rarely), but such people who do exist do not exhibit their knowledge publicly as such powers prove to be a hurdle on the path of spirituality.

“And those who don’t have this knowledge will promise you by charging an exorbitant fee. Such is the reality.

“There are many so-called commercial teachers existing on the planet today who have reached the stage wherein they have grasped this knowledge and with this self-discovery of knowledge they feel powerful, their ego is boosted and they come under the delusion that they are enlightened souls. They have even had very many spiritual experiences hypnotizing them to believe that they are truly enlightened souls.

“Unfortunately, Nikhil, such people are far from reality. Understanding what I have told you and experiencing what I have told you is where the main journey lies. It is only upon undertaking this journey that you will channelize your frequency with the Supreme and then discover and understand the true meaning of free will. It is this journey that the individual has to travel on his own. The guru can take you only to a point and that’s all, and it is in this journey that you will, if successful, be one with the Creator.”

“Please, my lord, explain this a little more,” I asked eagerly, and so Yama continued.

“You may have understood how to drive a car by reading a book or hearing the instructions from another driver, but actually sitting in a car and driving with ease are two different ends of the world.

“Those who have mastered how to drive the car are rare, the rest are all preachers who are preaching on how you can drive the car, having never even sat in one.

“Once when you sit in the driver’s seat and start driving, that’s when the journey to the Supreme will be in its final stage, and remember, you alone can be in that car. Such is the condition of the Creator. Many people give up because they think it’s very difficult and even get dejected. Unfortunately this is where the guru’s role becomes so crucial. If you have had a good instructor who himself is a master of driving then you will learn with ease. If you have had a master who is giving you bookish advice than how far can you possibly go? It's like the blind man being led by another blind man."

"Yes, my lord, this is now clear. But could you also tell me the relevance of Kundalini Yoga and its relevance with enlightenment? I do remember vaguely now how when I was young and jobless being very hard up on money that I was attracted by this person who offered to tell me how I could be extremely powerful, have lots of money and any women I wanted. But I could not afford the price; however, there was always this inclination of wanting to do it," I told Yama.

To this Yama replied, "Dear Nikhil, today there are two types of people who are indulging in things such as Kundalini Yoga, black magic, Vedic mantra cure, etc., etc. One is he who is seeking money, power, success, the women of his dreams, the spurned lover, overcoming their monetary problems, etc., etc., etc.

"The second is he who is looking for answers to finding a purpose and meaning to this life.

"For both the kinds of souls there are an equal number of people to take advantage of their mental agony. The reason I use the word agony is because irrespective of whether you are seeking God or money, your mind is disturbed in wanting to achieve that desire—and with desire there is disappointment.

"However, for the first set of people I can only say that they are doomed in the everlasting cycle of birth and death till its time.

"For the second, they are also doomed, till such time they do not realize what is the right path."

"So what happens then?" I asked, "Where is the solution?"

"Have patience, Mr. Nikhil, it is not just coincidence that I am here sitting with you. It is a part of the Creator's grand design. The last time I journeyed with anyone from your planet was a smart, young and extremely stubborn lad called Nachiketa."

"Yes, of course," I said, "I have read about it but always thought it was mythological. Do you mean all that really happened?"

"I am sitting with you right now, am I not?" Yama replied with a smile.

"True, my lord," I said, feeling stupid about the question I asked considering the circumstances under which I was in now. "But do tell me," I continued, "does Kundalini Yoga actually give one power and money as mentioned and commonly spoken of?"

"First of all let me tell you that this craving for power, money, etc. are thoughts arising from the mind of an ignorant soul. What is power and money for, when everything is already yours and your creation. Once you realize this you will find such cravings silly and those craving for it, sillier still.

"Imagine in your dream that you see yourself craving for money to the extent that you start getting frustrated and eventually commit suicide. Now once awake you will find it silly since it was just a dream. It is this awakening that a man must seek if at all he seeks anything.

"Till such time one desires something the law of karma will be there and with every action there will be a reaction. Once this desire is overcome after man realizes this world to be a dream and he one with the Creator he may then do anything he pleases and the law of karma will not touch him. This is what Krishna the avatar of Vishnu tried to preach, and such is the life that he lived.

"Where the kundalini is concerned, be rest assured anyone claiming to raise it for you is fooling the poor soul. Rest assured even the one who is claiming to do it for you has never experienced it himself.

"Ramakrishna Paramhans, Swami Lahiri Mahasaya, Sri Ramana Maharishi were amongst a few who had achieved this in recent times. Truly great were these souls. I bless them and they who were their disciples and further their disciples.

"There are mantras and rituals written in the scriptures that are done to get supernatural powers but such were applicable in another *yuga* and not apt for this *yuga* (*Kali Yuga*). This, my dear Nikhil, is the truth. So no matter how much you perform *yagnas* and sacrifices, they are not meant for this *yuga*.

"Let me tell you a story about a man who was struggling with life and was financially challenged. One day he met a person who said he could change everything for him. The poor soul was so desperate that he was willing to try anything and so after borrowing money he paid the astrologer and left it to him.

"Now this astrologer was a expert in astrology and was performing rituals for materialistic gains as mentioned and written in the ancient scriptures.

"And so the ritual was performed and that poor man became extremely rich and a devout follower of the astrologer, regularly donating exorbitant amounts of money to his ashram.

"To this same astrologer came another man, as his name had spread in fame. He emptied his pocket but unfortunately nothing happened.

"'Never mind,' said the astrologer, and assured him that he would perform a more powerful ritual. This continued for many such rituals, but nothing happened.

"Now Nikhil, understand what was happening," said Yama. "In the first case the poor man became rich not because of the astrologer but because his time had come. It was only coincidence that he had chanced upon the astrologer. In the second case the time had not come for the poor man to become rich monetarily and, therefore, any number of rituals performed by the astrologer were of no avail. One will find many such cases from where you have come.

"This happened despite the fact that the astrologer had mastered the rituals, the reason being, Nikhil, that the rituals are not applicable for this age."

"Then what is, my lord?"

"Soon, I shall tell you," Yama told me with assurance.

"However, till then understand what the relation with kundalini and spiritual awakening.

"When man is on the final journey alone as he must, he encounters a higher spiritual dimension. It is extremely important that the man at this stage has the correct interpretation of what must be achieved; otherwise the encounter with the awakening will never take place. That's why the guru has such an important place in the journey, so as to prepare the disciple for this very moment. Any person who has successfully achieved spiritual heights has traveled this journey alone. As had Christ and as had Lord Buddha under the bodhi tree and many more like them.

"I shall not spend time with you on the micro-understanding of different levels of the rising kundalini as it is available on any Internet search engine quite authentically, but I shall tell you what is *not* there.

"With these yogic practices as preached one cannot achieve awakening.

"The right and only way to achieve it in this age is as follows.

"The first is to follow any religion that you follow with the true spiritual interpretation of its preaching's. What is important is that Man must have faith. With the mercy of the Lord and the man's karma the Creator will soon show him the direction.

"The second was through the manifestation of a great soul called Maha-avatar Babaji, whose disciple was Lahiri Mahasaya. Through Maha-avatar Babaji was introduced the dead science as taught by Lord Krishna, the science of Kriya Yoga.

"However, even when taking the aid of these two or any other path there is one more path, an aspect that is a prerequisite without which it will not be possible: contemplation, introspection, and the art of rejection.

"The teachings of other great souls will also eventually pinpoint you to one or something similar to one of these directions.

"Irrespective, once Man travels on this path, the dormant power of his original being, that is to be of the Creator, starts dawning upon him. It is as if a king suffering from amnesia, living the life of a beggar, starts getting his memory back.

"To this there are various stages. As the memory starts coming back Man starts to realize his true nature. But this stage is extremely dangerous. As one starts to realize his true nature there is a tremendous energy that engulfs him making him believe that he has reached the end of the road. Each path provides the person with tremendous powers relevant to the materialistic world. Many falter at this stage. Many cannot comprehend this exposure and develop a massive ego when they have only reached the first stage, making them believe that they have reached the final stage.

"Such people are many, Nikhil, and they are the vultures I want you to educate mankind to be careful of."

"*I*, my lord? But I am dead and sitting with you in the astral world. How can I?"

"My dear Nikhil, let time determine and comprehend what is in store," spoke Yama.

"As the kundalini starts rising Man is exposed to many spiritual insights and power. However, these powers also come under the purview of karma till such time Man does not reach the final stage.

"Many people get drunk with this power, not wanting to go beyond. But soon this power is lost and the fall brings about tremendous destruction in its journey downward."

CHAPTER THREE

THE HIGHEST TRUTH

"Now listen, Nikhil, to the greatest secret of all. For man to travel the path he needs to understand the two aspects of the Creator. First is the dark aspect (energy in the formless state), and the second is the light from which all that is, was created. Now understand this light (Vishnu) which is the cause of creation emerged from the dark aspect of life in an inverted state, which means it was created within and not outside the dark energy which is why it is called the illusory world. Therefore, I will tell you that in light there is ignorance and in darkness there is illumination. This dark energy is Man's true nature and is seated in every creation. By saying 'dark' do not mistake it for negative energy, but that aspect which is nothingness. When one dissects any creation there will be a point of nothingness. It is from this nothingness (dark energy) that everything is created. As one peels an onion layer by layer till there comes a point of nothingness similarly man has to look within, with introspection and rejection till it reaches that point of nothingness. In Man this point is known medically as the mid-brain. If one may recount, in many scriptures there is great importance given to meditating within and between the eyebrows which is straight in line with the mid-brain. This mid-brain is also termed as third eye or the Eye of Shiva. Once this mid-brain gets activated it acts like a black hole. At this point man loses consciousness of this illusory world and experiences nothingness. Reaching this point is not the end but the start of the journey. From here now starts the revelation of the truth or, one may say the opening of the third eye. On this revelation also starts the awakening of the kundalini which is a journey through different gateways of this multidimensional world.

"Now understand, Nikhil, the awakening of the kundalini can only be done through introspection, contemplation and rejection of everything that comes in the path as the symbolic snake rises up the spine. As the snake climbs there will be many temptations that will need to be rejected. There will be great fears that will need to be overcome. As the snake climbs higher there will be a point where one will even have to reject the desire to understand the purpose of life. Moving still higher there will be point where he will even have to reject the desire of seeking the truth and bliss, and when finally there is rejection of everything that is, it will be at that moment, Nikhil, that man will find himself released from the bondage of the physical, astral and the casual world, and emerge as a free soul merged with the Creator, leaving no difference between the two. Such was Krishna's existence and such can be Man's.

"This, NIkhil, is the truth."

"But, my lord, do tell me when does Man reach that moment when the symbolic snake stirs and starts its climb."

"That, Nikhil, is the point when the guru has taught the disciple the art of contemplation, introspection and rejection, and such is the great importance of a guru—who, remember, need not be in physical form. So, tell mankind not to seek a guru, for when the time is right he will come to you in accordance with your karma. Till then there will pain and there will be pleasure. Till then, there will be birth and there will be death; till then, Nikhil, there will be gain and there will be loss. Man must learn to embrace them both, till the moment comes."

"But, my lord, having had reached the stage of a free soul, why would Man want to continue to live on this or any of the planes? To this doubt in my mind, my lord, please guide me as to why enlightened souls like Christ or Lord Buddha continued to live this life."

"That, Nikhil, is free will. What we see as the suffering of Christ was his free will to demonstrate mankind's suffering. Lord Buddha tried to show Man that realization can happen only through introspection and contemplation as he did under the Bodhi Tree and not by taking hardships and escapism."

"But Lord Buddha sacrificed all his attachments and escaped in the night, didn't he, my lord?" I asked.

"Yes, Nikhil, he did, and he also tried all sorts of yogic practices and tantra and hardships, but did any of that give him enlightenment?

"Finally it was only contemplation through the art of rejection that he emerged enlightened under the Bodhi Tree as had also Christ. Lord Buddha having realized this spoke not of worshiping him but tried to speak and preach about the importance of introspection as have all great souls.

"Many people having reached very high levels do find life meaningless, and through powers achieved, can give up their bodies voluntarily. But many in such cases do not emerge as free souls but are manifested into high astral or casual bodies. In such cases when lacking in the right levels of subtle introspection somewhere in finding this life meaningless he is somewhere seeking something meaningful, which makes him come under the purview of karma thereby not letting him emerge as a free soul. Such is the level of subtle introspection that even the gods have failed to realize.

"Many great souls have faltered with the rise of the symbolic snake, even the likes of Vishwamitra (who gifted mankind with the greatest mantra, known as the Gayatri) got distracted.

"However, he did recover to realize the grave mistake he had made and moved forward. Many such stories have been told over the centuries to warn Man who walks on this path."

"Could you tell me about the Gayatri Mantra, my lord?" I asked, the hunger for knowledge growing more and more within me.

Lord Yama smiled at me, and lovingly told me, "My dear Nikhil, what I have spoken to you about all this while is nothing but the Gayatri Mantra.

"Many speak of it, many people talk of the power it bestows, but this is that one mantra that even the great gods have failed to comprehend.

"It is not the mantra that is important, Nikhil, it is the philosophy of the mantra that holds the essence of the power behind it, and that is the philosophy that I have shared with you. But remember, just understanding it is not enough. One has to continue with perseverance and wait for that moment when the time is ripe, and the symbolic snake stirs and starts its journey upward. It is the philosophy of this mantra that must be in the heart as the snake climbs. It is only on completion of that journey that you will emerge as one with the Creator. Remember also, Nikhil, that this symbolic snake is nothing but the journey of revelation of one's true nature accompanied by deviations of desire and everything that is there which needs to be rejected.

"And also remember that for this moment one need not run to the jungle or any ashram or undertake any form of yoga or tantric practices. It can happen in the midst of your worldly affairs perfectly naturally as you go on with your daily chores."

"But, lord, I am slightly confused. On the one hand you are saying not to give up anything. On the other hand you are mentioning that one has to reject everything so as to emerge as a free soul. Could you guide me on this doubt, my lord?" I asked.

Lovingly, Yama continued.

"My dear Nikhil, if one were to comprehend the Gayatri, it speaks about creation of the three worlds. From a source where there was an explosion of the glorious light, defined as *Bhargo* in the Gayatri. The first manifestation, symbolically called Vishnu. This manifestation (Vishnu) has many attributes such as being full, the knower of all, knowing whom nothing more needs to be known; pure bliss, the one with divine wisdom, all-powerful, full of strength, wealth and dispassion; all-pervading, eternal, infinite, he in me and I in him.

"Now introspect on the last sentence. He is in me and I in him. This gives the first hint of maya. The dream world. Everything that was created was in thought; dreams within dreams; the creation of the three worlds; one within the other. That's why Man also dreams because of that quality of the Creator. Remember when I told you through Vishnu was created

Brahma and then the casual worlds and so on and so forth. All this is nothing but a dream within a dream.

"Now the question arises as to what was the source of the creation of Vishnu. To which the answer is defined in the Gayatri as '*Tat*,' meaning that from which all was created. That, Nikhil, is the formless aspect of Vishnu, the dark energy (Shakti) about which I have spoken to you before, the one without form, the ultimate truth called Brahman to which is ascribed in the scriptures as 'Neti Neti'—'Not this, Not that,' since it is beyond description."

"So, my lord," I continued with fascination, "this also means that Vishnu is a manifestation and, therefore, also subject to destruction."

"Yes," replied Yama, "the death of Brahma is the awakening of Vishnu into his formless state.

"Now understand that the cause of creation was a reflection of all the qualities of the formless. However, with ignorance one forgot the purpose of his existence as did the gods because of false ego, thereby coming under the purview of karma. The reason I told you to educate mankind not to escape but to take bliss in the gift of life was because that was the cause for the formless Creator's creation. And the reason I asked you to reject everything was because that is your true nature. 'Neti Neti': Not this, Not that'."

CHAPTER FOUR

WHY ME?

"Why me, my lord? I was just a ordinary man in life. I did not even think much of spirituality. As a matter of fact, my lord," I spoke with tears rolling down my eyes, "I even thought of people seeking spirituality as escapists. A justification for people who have failed in life, and for those who were rich a justification for not being able to take the pressure of life. I had just one word for them, my lord: 'Escapists.' Yet here I am being told the greatest secret of our existence not even known to the gods in heaven. Why me, my lord, why me?" I said, falling down on my knees not being able to understand anything of what was happening to me now.

Lord Yama held me up as a loving father would to his child who had fallen, and thus spoke.

"My dear Nikhil, desire is an extremely dangerous thing and so is this illusion of life. The greatest of souls have fallen into this trap. You, my dear, were amongst them."

"I don't understand, my lord," I said, finding it more confusing now.

"In your life before your previous one, Nikhil, you were a very advanced yogi, not a free soul but very advanced. You went to great heights of spiritual evolution: nonetheless, despite your greatness you succumbed to the trap of the illusory world and became a victim of the very same dangers that you had overcome and preached to your disciples one of whom was a child named Sanyal. It was on his request that I have granted you this moment.

"Despite all that Man has achieved or gained, the Creator gifted Man with one more moment to overcome his ignorance, which is to be made at the time of death.

"What a man thinks at the time of death is with what he is rewarded. One may have lived a life of a thief but at the time of death if he thinks of the gods, he shall go to them. Or one may have been a great yogi, but at the time of death if he thinks of seeking power he shall be born in a totally different environment having nothing to do with spirituality at all. But, of course, his karma of his past continues to play a vital role and eventually will guide him to come back to the correct path which could take many lifetimes.

"However, it is not as easy as it sounds. Many ignorant souls may say, OK, in that case let me indulge in all sorts of impure activities and at the moment of death I shall think of the gods, but that is not to happen. This thought, to come to your mind, requires extremely high levels of discipline and a natural thought process that has to come from within. One cannot train himself to do it even if one creates the right environment.

"There are many circumstances under which a man may die. Even if one may know death is imminent as he is suffering from cancer and makes arrangements for recitation of the Bhagwad Gita, but at the time of death he may be dreaming of being with his son and so he will be manifested back to the physical plane close to his son. Or if his son is dead then close to the re-manifestation of his son."

"Are all these people born back in the same plane?" I asked.

"As I told you before, Nikhil, at the moment of death, depending on your thought you get manifested in any location as there are end numbers of such multidimensional worlds. However, in most of the cases due to deep-rooted desire of attachments after a period of rest one is manifested into similar circumstances. Who was your grandfather today could be manifested as your son tomorrow and so on and so forth. Even the interactions you have had with people today have been the same people that you have had interactions with in the past, such is the monotony of life, like a wheel going round and round just the bodies are discarded for new ones only to be discarded again. Even the situations that you face today are in accordance with the past. Let us say, for example, you have a boss who has made your life miserable. The reason you are in this situation today is because at some point in this or your past life you had done the same to him. You may have a lover who leaves you in the midst of your relationship for another man, leaving you extremely depressed; rest assured the same act had been demonstrated by you in the past. To this fact there are no two views.

"This is the reason why in the scriptures it has been mentioned to be kind to all, for what one sows is what one reaps. But, of course, man in this *yuga* is too ignorant to see this factor, as also you could not, despite your greatness in your life before the previous. Such is the power of maya (illusion)."

"What happened to me, my lord?" I asked, really amazed that I was a yogi with a spiritually evolved soul and yet be reborn under circumstances where I had nothing to do with spirituality.

With a smile on his face, Yama asked me, "Do you really wish to know?"

I said yes, but with a little hesitation knowing well as how on the last occasion he transported me back to live my life to witness old age.

"My lord," I asked, "how many years will I have to live that moment?"

"Don't bother about the time," Yama spoke, "once you wake up it will feel only like a couple of seconds. Just like a dream. Just as you now perceive your previous life. It felt only like a couple of seconds, didn't it?" Yes, it did, I thought. A whole life on earth to wake up into realizing it was only a couple of seconds. And how seriously and ignorantly we take our lives: truly amazing, I thought.

"Give me your hands," Yama commanded as I hesitantly held them out.

Holding my hands, I started getting that sinking feeling. I was almost getting used to traveling back and forth in time zones. This one was going to be my life before the previous.

CHAPTER FIVE

SEX AND THE SWAMI

"Guruji, Guruji!" Sanyal, my beloved and youngest disciple of 8 years came running into my room almost out of breath.

"How many times have I told you, Sanyal, to stop getting excited? There is nothing in this world that requires such urgency: you need to curb and conserve your energy," I reprimanded Sanyal.

"But, Guruji," continued Sanyal, but before he could complete I told him lovingly, "I know, Sanyal, Suryananda has arrived at the ashram."

"Yes, Guruji, but how did you know?" Holding his hands I made him sit on my lap and lovingly whispered into his ears, "I know everything." He hugged me, and started running away shouting and making the other disciples aware. "Surya dada has arrived, Surya dada has arrived."

As I looked at him, I was reminded of a rabbit.

I still remember, six years back while meditating in the ashram, my guru appeared before me. The instructions from him were to proceed to Calcutta immediately. On my arrival, Guruji continued, "Violence will erupt and many people will be killed. Over there you will find a child of 2 years sitting in front of the body of his dead parents with a scar under his left foot. You are to pick him up and raise him in the ashram with utmost care as I did to you. Tutor him with love as you would to the king of heaven who has lost his memory."

I immediately left and in accordance with the instructions found him in the exact location as instructed from my guru.

How time had passed. Through my yogic powers I knew who he was but could not reveal the same to him or to anyone else. It would have to be his journey: such was the only way.

As I sat there thinking, Suryananda entered and bowed down before me touching my feet for blessings.

Suryananada, my first disciple, was advancing rapidly in his spiritual progress but I knew that it would be many more lifetimes before he must emerge victorious.

"What brings you here, Surya?" I asked, knowing fully well the reason why he had come.

"Gurudev, Swami Abhedanada has returned from his travel, and has sent this *prasad* for you."

"Of course; you may keep it in that corner."

I knew very well that Swami Abhedanada could travel in time and manifest himself anywhere, but the purpose of sending Surya out here was for his protection. Upon Surya was looming death and, till such time the cloud of death did not pass him he could only be protected under my presence. There would be two more such occasions. If he survived them I knew he would live to be 100. But it was important that he should overcome his karma on Earth and move on to higher astral planets to overcome his karma there. If death caught up with him before that, he could be lost forever.

It was my purpose to continue my life on Earth as instructed from my guru to serve the lost souls guiding them to higher levels. At times, recently, the thought of giving up my body and joining my guru in the higher planes had started creeping into me. I knew this was dangerous: the mind was manifesting desires into me. I needed to be careful.

It was noon when we all gathered in the garden, offered prayers and proceeded for lunch.

Sanyal came and sat on my lap, as he would insist on having food from the same plate as I did and, he would have it in no other way as long as I was in the ashram. We continued chit-chatting, with Surya talking about worldly affairs and sharing his experience of Calcutta.

"There is talk about independence, freeing India from the clutches of British rule," spoke Surya.

"The only independence you should be worried about, Surya, is independence from the clutches of ignorance. If you focus more on that the better it will be for you," I replied.

"I am sorry, Gurudev," Surya replied, feeling perhaps that his comment had made me angry.

"Don't be sorry, Surya. It is not as if worldly affairs are bad, but the danger is that before we know it, maya (illusion) grips us and we are lost forever in the cycle of birth and death."

"Guruji," Sanyal interrupted, "what is death?"

"Finish the rice then I will tell you," I replied.

"I am planning to leave for Calcutta tomorrow," Surya continued.

"What's the hurry?" I asked, "Stay here till Durga Puja. We will require your help and, of course, with your city knowledge you could help us organize it better."

I saw his eyes light up, and Sanyal started jumping in my lap screaming, "Surya dada is going to stay! Surya dada is going to stay!"

As much as Surya had not wanted to leave the Ashram three years back, it was important that he moved on to spread the teachings in the modern cities that were coming up. I had to forcibly ask him to go to live in Calcutta for higher education under Abhedananda's guidance with instructions of visiting the ashram once a year for not more than two days. His attachment to me was becoming a hindrance in his spiritual growth.

There was a lot of activity in the ashram as Durga Puja was approaching and a lot of preparations were to be made. I personally did not give much to idol worshipping but, at the same time did not want to enforce my views on others. Let them decide for themselves.

After my guru's departure each of his disciples were given specific roles. There were five of us. I was given charge of the running the ashram. As was the responsibility, I tried to let everything be as my guru had. There was much fanfare associated with Durga Puja. I also had to ensure that the idols be made under specific instructions for which I had to periodically travel to another town 50 km from the ashram. There would also be many visitors, so things had to be well planned.

By the time the sun had risen I had finished my bath and meditation and was ready to leave for Chunanagar, where the idol was being made. The delivery was to be done in a week from now.

On reaching Chunanagar the tonga stopped outside Subroto's house, who was the idol maker. As I entered he rushed to greet me, touching my feet, seated me comfortably and called out to Paaro to bring some snacks and tea for me. "Who is Paaro?" I asked.

"Gurudev, she is my niece who is visiting us from Calcutta."

"Aaah, puja holidays. I didn't know you had a niece, Subroto."

Gurudev, this is the first time she is visiting. Please make yourself comfortable. I just have go to the market to get some material for the finishing touches."

"Why don't you take my tonga? That way you will return faster."

"Thank you, Gurudev," saying which he left.

Closing my eyes I tried to get some rest, just when I could feel someone touch my feet and whisper, "Guruji, please have your tea."

As I opened my eyes, it fell upon the revealing cleavage of Paaro's breast as she slowly stood up after touching my feet. I quickly glanced away only to look at her face which made my heart skip a beat. She was the most beautiful woman I had ever set my eyes on.

"Guruji, please have your tea, its getting cold," she repeated as I found myself hypnotized staring into her face.

"Yes, yes, thank you," I said, quickly composing myself.

As I sipped my tea she said in a sing-song voice, "Did you like it, Guruji?"

"Like what?" I asked, still trying to recover from the sight of her cleavage.

"But, of course, the tea, Guruji. Was there anything else that you liked?" she asked, smiling sheepishly.

"Yes, yes, it's very good."

"Can I press your feet, Guruji? My father tells me that if we serve holy men that way we will have a good life, and you have come from a long journey," she continued.

"Thank you, that's very kind of you, but I'll be fine," I replied, wondering what it would feel like when she pressed my feet with her tender hands.

Insisting without asking for further permission she fell on her knees and started pressing my feet, once again revealing her cleavage to me.

As much as I tried I could not take my eyes off it. As she sensuously massaged my feet she gently asked me, knowing fully well that I was staring at her breasts, "Are you enjoying it?" and I replied shamelessly, "Yes, it feels very relaxing."

Slowly and steadily she started moving her hands upward toward my calves. I could feel the hardness in my groin.

"Enjoying it?" she kept repeating and I just kept saying yes.

She was now edging toward my thighs when we could hear the trotting of horses, as the tonga came to a halt at the entrance.

She hurriedly got up and left, giggling, leaving me red-faced and dumbstruck.

What did I just do, I thought, totally confused with my action.

But before I could think more Subroto entered and guided me to the back of his house to show me how he was progressing with the idols.

My mind was anywhere but with him or the idols. I just continued thinking about Paaro, her touch, her sensuality and somewhere as much as I was trying to distract my thoughts away from her I could not deny what a great moment I had just experienced.

Subroto noticed that I was lost in thought and interrupted me by asking if everything was OK.

"Yes. Yes, please continue."

"Unfortunately, Guruji, some of the material has gotten over and can be available only in Calcutta."

"So what is the problem?" I asked.

"I am unable to leave my niece alone and the supplier says that it will be a couple of days before the supply reaches him."

Now surely that was a problem, I thought. The puja was set to start in a week from now.

"Dada, I can stay on my own," came Paaro's voice from behind.

"Keep quiet, you are just a child!" Subroto shouted back.

"I am 18 now," Paaro replied, now coming toward us.

"Don't you have manners, speaking like that in front of Guruji?" Subroto said, getting angry.

I don't know what made me say it, but I interfered and said, "Why doesn't she stay at the ashram?"

"But, Guruji, it would be so much of inconvenience to you," Subroto insisted.

"Not at all," I replied, thinking about her hands on my thighs. "But why don't you ask Paaro?"

Quickly, she replied, "Yes. Yes, I would love to, I have heard so much about it. Is it really as beautiful as people say it is?"

"Why don't you come and see for yourself, if that is OK with your Dada?"

"Guruji, you are too kind," Subroto replied.

Instead of cursing myself and feeling guilty I was feeling ecstatic, looking forward to our meeting again.

"Well then, that settles it. I will send the tonga tomorrow to pick her and also send some advance."

Saying this I requested for leave.

Once I left there were other things that needed to be purchased and on the journey back there was nothing that I could do except to think about Paaro.

As the tonga entered the ashram it was already dark. Sanyal and others came out to help in unloading the goods I had purchased. Sanyal quietly pulled my kurta as a coded signal to get confirmation if I had got anything special for him. Quietly, I assured him and he ran away knowing very well that I would give it to him when no one else was around.

At dinner I announced to everyone that we would be having a guest tomorrow. "Who is he, Guruji?" Surya asked.

"The sculptor's niece. She has come from Calcutta and wishes to spend some time in the ashram. She can be accommodated in the guest house in the ladies' section," I replied

"I shall see to it personally, Guruji," Surya promptly replied.

For a moment I wished Surya was not there. She was young and attractive as was Surya. What if she wanted Surya instead of me, I thought.

"What was happening to me? I must correct myself. Maybe I should have not allowed her to come here at all?"

That night as I sat down for meditation, I just could not get myself to concentrate and chose to sleep rather than meditate.

The next morning before doing anything I made the tonga depart for Subroto's house, my heart beating fast with the excitement of seeing her.

I stood in front of the mirror and wondered what could have excited her about this man in saffron. I was 35 and she 18, I thought. Never had I given any importance to my looks but, taking a closer look I thought myself to be quite attractive. I was clean-shaven, perhaps if I had a beard like many others it would have scared her off. I was well built. Yes, I was quite attractive even as compared with anyone else in the ashram. Even amongst my guru's five disciples.

"Oh my God!" I thought, for the first time the thought dawning upon me. What would they think of me when they realized what I had done. I needed to protect myself immediately. I rushed into my room and immediately started recitation of the mantra that provides the shield of protection. This way they would not be able to contact or know what I was doing even with their telepathic powers. We often did this while going into long durations of meditation so that no vibration interfered so as not to disturb the meditation.

For the first time I was using my powers for materialistic gain. Just this one time, I thought. She will soon go away and I will perform penance, I consoled myself, giving justification for my act.

Once the rites were complete, I was relieved no one had come to know about this yet. I was now safe at least for some time.

It was lunchtime when I was informed that the lady had come and put up comfortably in the guest house.

"Good," I said wanting to meet her right away, but showing any sense of excitement would alert everyone, especially Surya. How I wished he was not here.

"Take good care of her, and I will meet her at 5 o'clock at the prayers," I told Surya to convey the message.

As the evening prayers got over, everyone went about their way and there she was standing in front of me, alone at last.

"So how are you liking the ashram?" I asked, trying hard to keep myself composed.

"Oh Guruji, it's wonderful," she replied.

Indeed it was, built on 20 acres of land, it truly was beautiful. My guru had personally overlooked the construction of the ashram, the funds for which came freely from a local landlord.

"I am being treated like a princess out here," she continued in her sing-song voice.

As we strolled we found ourselves secluded from everyone's sight. Purposely, I had guided her there so that no one else could see us.

"But, Guruji, you are so busy out here," she said.

"Unfortunately, I am, Paaro, but Surya can show you around," I replied, hoping I had never mentioned it.

"No, no, Guruji, how I wish I could spend more time with you," she said, to my great relief.

"The last time when we met, Guruji, I could not serve you well. I wish I had more time to show you how much better I can do."

As she spoke these words I could feel the hardness rising again.

"Will I get your time, Guruji?" she asked teasingly.

"Time for what?" I asked trying to play along.

"That, Guruji, I will show you when you give me your time." As she said these words she came very close to me, held my hands and placed them on her breasts and asked, "Can you feel my heartbeat, Gurudev?"

"Yes. Yes, I can," I replied hoping this moment would never end. Her heart indeed was beating very fast, as was mine.

"My heart beats for you," she whispered in my ears, "I knew that, Gurudev, the moment I set my eyes on you." She continued speaking at the same time guiding my hands to massage her breasts.

Her breasts felt so soft, I almost felt like tearing the blouse that came in-between and kissing them in the flesh.

"I'll see you tonight in your room. Leave it open for me," I whispered in her ear and parted ways lest anyone see us.

As I went back to my room I sat there trembling with the experience I had just had. All my life I had led the life of a *brahmachari*, never having experienced sex, never ever having even desired to do it, and here I was, now suddenly finding it the most exciting thing in life.

I was still wondering whether I should go tonight. With my powers I could ensure no one in the ashram would ever know. With my powers I could put the guards and all the ladies in the guest house go into a deep state of rest: they would not even hear an explosion if it went off outside their very own doors.

"Yes. Yes, all that can be done, but must I go," I kept contemplating.

It was 7 p.m. and now dinnertime. After dinner we all sat down as was routine and spoke about any incidents or issues related to the ashram or anything that anyone wanted to discuss at all. My thoughts, however, were only focused on Paaro.

By 10 p.m. everyone had gone off to sleep. With my special powers I just made them go off to sleep a little more deeply and decided finally that I would go to meet Paaro. I was now too frequently using my spiritual powers for personal gain, and realized how dangerous this could be. I was indeed treading on extremely dangerous grounds.

As I reached the guest house the guards were fast asleep. I walked into the ladies' section and found myself standing outside Paaro's door. With some hesitation I knocked on the door. As I did, the door opened and I realized that Paaro must have left it open. The candles were still burning and I could see Paaro lying down on her bed with her eyes wide open.

As she saw me she got up and came running toward me and held me, whispering, "Oh Guruji, thank God you have come."

I was feeling a little embarrassed but, at least it was clear to both of us as to why I had come; however, I was at a loss on how to take it further.

She comfortably held my hand and guided me to the bed and offered me a paan which I declined.

"Guruji, are you feeling comfortable?" she asked lifting my finger and sensuously taking it inside her mouth massaging it with her tongue, then each finger one by one.

"Please lie down, Guruji," she told me, helping me at the same time to get into a comfortable position.

"Paaro, can you please not call me Guruji at least for now?" I requested her, feeling somewhat guilty about it.

Like a snake she said, "Sssssshhhhhhh, Guruji, don't speak!"

I spoke no further. This was truly a unique experience.

She sensuously lifted my kurta and started kissing my lips, circling them with her tongue and then releasing them in a continuous process. With her fingers at the same time she slowly massaged me between my thighs, undoing my dhoti at the same time. I felt like exploding but kept in control. I had to enjoy this for as long as it took. Soon, I found myself lying down without any clothes, and her lips slowly discovering every part of my body.

"Tell me, Swami, are you likening it?"

Moaning with pleasure I replied, "Oh Paaro, don't stop!"

"Swami, I will do anything for you," and getting on top of me she now asked me to undo her blouse. Fumbling and not having the patience I just tore it and saw the beauty of her breasts staring into me. I caressed them tenderly discovering them bit by bit. With a forceful action I now got up, making her lie down with me on top undressing her from below. I knew she was a virgin, by misusing my powers yet again. I kissed her breasts and feeling the hardness of her nipples I suckled them with her moaning in pleasure. She held me by my hair and pushed me down toward her thighs. I moved further down and kissed her toes as she had done with my fingers. Slowly, I moved up toward her calves and then her thighs licking and probing them with my tongue like a possessed wild animal. I moved further up toward her stomach which felt warm as I buried my face into the soft flesh and with my hands massaged her breasts and nipples. As I moved toward her lips I tried to insert my hardness into her, fumbling at first. "No, no, Swami, not like that," she spoke gently as she held my hardness and directed it towards her tunnel of love. At first I found it difficult, her moaning was getting louder and louder. With a great thrust I pushed myself in, making her scream so loudly with pain that I had to cover her mouth with my hands to subdue the scream. Once inside I started gaining momentum as would a rider on a horse. My movement and hers were slowly getting synchronized into a perfect rhythm as if naturally. Her screams of pain started to turn into sounds of pleasure. "Let me come on top, Swami," she shyly whispered. I complied with her wish and switching positions she was now the rider and I the horse. As she moved her hips up and down her breasts were bouncing as if teasing me. I held them and moved toward them hungrily. With momentum came a strange feeling. There were very many great experiences that I had discovered, but this was different. Each experience was different as was this. I could feel something about to erupt, and the expressions took form in sounds of pleasure increasing in pitch and volume as did hers. I once again pinned her down with me on top and it was like hysteria, as both our movements gained momentum and with a final scream our bodies convulsed and then there was silence, just the sound of heavy breathing that comes with exhaustion. I collapsed on top of her and we lay there holding each others' hands till I knew that it was time for me to go back.

"Please don't go, Swamiji," she purred into my ears, tears rolling down her eyes.

"I must leave now, my love, but know that this is just the beginning. I will always be there for you," I replied, wondering how much of that would be true.

It was 3 a.m. when I walked back to my room, realizing that I already wanted to go back to Paaro.

That day everything continued as was routine. There was much excitement but, for me the only excitement was wanting to be with Paaro.

I had changed, I knew that, I could feel it in my heart and knew that I was in love with her. I continued to misuse my powers, this time to understand the art of giving pleasure to women as did the gods know in heaven.

I met Paaro after the evening prayers and told her to wait for me that night and, with those words I could see the radiance on her face which was otherwise looking tired with perhaps the lack of sleep.

That night we met again and this time I was prepared with confidence and knowledge only known to the gods.

Such was the experience Paaro had that she fainted, making me realize that the human body had its limitations.

I knew this would be the last night as her uncle would be back and I would have to make her depart tomorrow itself.

"Listen, Paaro. Come back here during the pujas with your Dada. Once you depart for Calcutta I will make arrangements to come there."

"Swami, will there ever be a time when we can always be together?"

"I wish for that too, but give me some time to work things out," I told her and left with a heavy heart.

I did not go to see her off the next day, but watched from a distance as she kept looking around to see any sign of me.

As the days went by I was overcome with grief from the desire of wanting to meet her but restrained myself, hoping I would get over it.

The day came when Subroto arrived with the idols and there were great celebrations as they were installed and given the final touches. When the time was right I approached Subroto and, seeing me he bowed down, touching my feet.

"Truly you have done a wonderful job," I told him trying to create a situation where I could ask him about Paaro.

"Guruji, this is all because of your blessing," he replied humbly.

"No, Subroto, don't thank me for your skills: if at all, thank the Lord."

"As you say, Guruji, but for us you are God," he continued passionately.

I wondered if he would say that if he knew about Paaro and me.

"Anyway, Subroto, how is your niece? I do hope she had a good time in the ashram," I asked, wanting to hear about her.

"Oh Guruji, she is missing it and was insisting on coming, but I am so busy that I just don't have time."

"Oh well, how then will she enjoy her holiday?" I asked, thinking that maybe I could corner him into sending her here again.

"I too am feeling bad, Gurudev, but the work load has increased so much that it is difficult for me to even spend any time with her, let alone show her around."

"Then why doesn't she spend more time here?" I asked, wondering if he would take the bait.

"Guruji, you are indeed kind, but you have already done so much," he said.

"Oh, it's nothing," I replied, knowing that I was almost there into making him say yes.

As I was waiting for his reply some of the disciples came to me requesting me to come to the temple for consent on certain matters.

How I cursed them, knowing that I had lost my game plan.

But I knew that I must not give up, There were ten days to go for the last day of the festival and on the eleventh day she would leave for Calcutta.

Something had to be done, thinking of which I followed my disciples toward the temple.

As the day went by, one of the disciples came to me asking for the payment that needed to be made to Subroto.

With relief I found the solution to my problem. "Shantanu, tell Subroto that due to my being very busy right now, I shall make the payment tomorrow since I am going to Chunanagar."

"As you wish, Guruji," Shantanu bowed and departed to give him the message.

With great relief I knew now what had to be done.

The next morning I departed with the excitement of seeing Paaro again.

As the horse halted before Subroto's house I saw Paaro rushing to receive me, shouting out loudly, "Dada, Dada! Guruji has come!"

She came and touched my feet, her face glowing with radiance as a flower blooms with the onset of the first shower of the monsoons. My heart ached to hold her but how could I.

Subroto came and, touching my feet said, "Guruji, what was the hurry? The money could have waited."

"No, no," I replied, "It is festive season and besides, your niece is here, you need to show her around."

Paaro quickly responded, "Guruji, Dada has no time for me."

Subroto was quick in reprimanding Paaro, and told her to make some tea. As we sat down I spent some time in praising Subroto's work and handed him the money.

On counting the money, Subroto said, "Guruji, you have given a lot more than what I had asked for."

"Subroto, for the past so many years you have been making the idols for the ashram as your father did before you. And yet you still charge the same amount as you did 10 years ago. It is not as if I am not aware of the rising prices, Subroto, yet you sacrifice and even spend from your own pocket."

With these words Subroto had tears in his eyes and touched my feet. Just then Paaro came with the tea and joined us in our conversation.

"So, Subroto, tell me, why is Paaro complaining?" I asked, trying to lighten the conversation.

"Yes, yes, Dada, tell Guruji why I am complaining," Paaro prompted Subroto.

"What can I say, Guruji? I have taken upon myself more work than I can handle and that too with no help," he said with a sorry look on his face.

"Why can't I stay in the ashram? There is so much there to do and what a beautiful place it is," came Paaro's prompt reply.

"Keep quiet," Subroto scolded her.

"As a matter of fact, Subroto, Paaro is correct. There is indeed a lot of work in the ashram; we could always do with additional help," I said, trying once again into cornering Subroto.

"But, Guruji," Subroto tried to say something before which I stood up and said, "No buts, Subroto, she has come here for her holiday and she is our guest: the rest is your choice. I must leave now, Subroto, as much work needs to be done."

"O Guruji, please don't leave just yet. At least have some snacks. I will bring her tomorrow, Guruji, and how can I possibly thank you enough for that kindness that you have shown?"

"But remember, Paaro, along with your holiday you will also have to work in the ashram," I said, trying to create the right balance.

"Have you heard Guruji? Work properly in the ashram," Subroto told Paaro, and then humbly told me, "Guruji, you must scold her if she doesn't work."

"I promise, Dada, I will work very hard."

Having finished the snacks I requested for leave. As I was getting into the tonga, Subroto, touching my feet, told me he would leave for the ashram first thing in the morning.

"Why do you bother? The tonga will be coming every day for supplies from tomorrow. Once the supplies have been taken it can come and pick Paaro up tomorrow."

"As you wish, Guruji."

With these words I departed, the excitement of being with Paaro once again in my heart.

It was almost sunset the next day when Paaro arrived. We met in the evening in the temple amongst many others. I could not have a private moment with her since so many people were there, but somehow I had to give her the message to wait for me that night. I did get my moment and, from that day on till the last day we met every night. Each night a new discovery and, each night I found myself drowning deeper in love.

It was the last night we were spending together. There was sadness in both our hearts and I knew that this was not how I wanted it to end.

I had made my decision that we had to be together for as long as I lived.

Gathering courage I asked Paaro if she wanted to spend her life with me.

"Swami, I can think of no one else," she replied, leaving me to wonder how I could make this possible.

"We will have to run away, Paaro: under the circumstances there is no other way."

"I will follow you till death, Swami," she answered, the time being right for me to now share my plan with her.

"In a week from now on the 14th of this month I shall meet you in Calcutta. Meet me at the Kali Temple at 2 p.m. From there we will proceed to Bombay and spend our lives together. Bring with you only the basic necessities." Having said this I wondered whether it was the right thing I was doing, but my heart would have it no other way.

"Oh Swami, will you really come? I don't know how I will even spend that one week without you," she replied, holding on to me as if never wanting to let go.

As the next day arrived she departed and I knew that many arrangements were to be made. The thing that was bothering me the most was how I could break the news to my guru.

I undid my shield of protection and now had to wait till they came to me instead of I going to them.

As the days passed I was surprised why my guru, or his other disciples had not confronted me till now. It was not possible that they would have not discovered my intentions. There were only two days left before I would leave for Calcutta. There was the ashram to take care of. Surya was safe now, but the sadness of leaving Sanyal was heavy in my heart.

I was surprised at my levels of emotion, but I knew this was a reaction that was resulting from my materialistic desires. Soon enough I was also aware that I would lose all my powers. But all this was nothing as compared to my love for Paaro, I thought.

That night after dinner as I entered my room I saw standing in all his splendor, my guruji. I was scared and ashamed at what I had done but, this moment of confrontation was imminent.

"Guruji," I spoke, and rushed to touch his feet.

"Aah, Nachiketa, it's been a while since I have seen you, but why the sadness on seeing me?" he asked tenderly.

"I have shamed you, Guruji," I spoke, still at his feet.

With warmth, my guru lifted me and said, "My dearest Nachiketa, you have not shamed me, or anyone: you have only deviated from your path. Had it been anyone else one could scold him as one does to a child, but you, Nachiketa, knew what was right but chose to follow a different path. If a man knows he's falling into a well and chooses to continue despite there being a rope to hold on to and climb back, what can I say of a man such as him."

I had no reply to his words and continued to stand in front of him with my head bowed in shame.

"My dearest of dearest," continued my guru, "it was not as if I did not know what you were doing; your protective shield has no effect on me, but I chose not to interfere. Do you wish to know why?"

I did not respond to his question with either a yes or a no.

"Oh Nachiketa, now stop behaving like a child who has been caught stealing. Paaro is indeed a very pretty girl," he said shocking me with his reply.

"But Guruji," I replied, not knowing what to say.

"Aah, the little child now speaks," he taunted me.

"The reason, Nachiketa, I did not stop you is because had I stopped you then or for that matter now, then your mind would never let you rest. You would have always cursed yourself, leaving you to be neither a man of the materialist world nor one of the spiritual world.

"You follow your instinct, live your life till you feel that you are ready to come here once again, and when you do—as I am sure you will—then work toward your goal with sincerity."

There was something different about my guru, as if he had discovered something new, an unknown truth, of this I was sure but also knew that I was not worthy of being shared that secret anymore.

"So tell me, Nachiketa, what are your plans for in Bombay."

"Guruji, I have not really thought about it."

"Aaah, the blind lover," he replied, taunting me once again.

"Do you know, Nachiketa, you were my favorite disciple?"

"No, Gurudev," I replied

"It saddens me to lose you, but such is way of the Lord," Guruji told me, looking somewhere lost in thought.

"Well," Guruji continued, "Abhi will take over the responsibility of the ashram; he will join you tomorrow and so make the announcement in his presence. It will be announced to all that you are going for a long journey to the Himalayas for higher spiritual progress: at least let's make your exit with some dignity and celebration. Also, you will receive two parcels tomorrow, one for you and one for Paaro."

He held me affectionately, and told me that he must now take leave.

As his body began to dematerialize his final words were words of warning.

"Nachiketa, as my body dematerializes all your powers will be over. You will come strongly under the purview of karma, so be warned of the downfall."

As guruji vanished, it left me worried with the road that lay ahead.

The next day Surya came to me with two suitcases, saying someone had delivered them for me.

"Leave them next to the bed," I replied, "and send Sanyal to me."

"Yes, Guruji," he said, bowing, and left.

I went to the suitcases. As I opened the first one I saw saris and jewelry meant for Paaro.

Tears rolled down my eyes. As I opened the second it had clothes for me. Not the regular clothes but those which were worn in the modern cities of today. There was also an envelope with money in it. Lots of money.

As tears continued rolling down my eyes, Sanyal entered, and seeing me as I was came running to me and asked, "Guruji, why the tears?"

Wiping them off I told Sanyal it was nothing and holding him, I made him sit in my lap and told him, "My dear child, there is something important that I must tell you."

"What is it, Guruji?"

"There comes a time when a person has to move on, as must I."

"Are you going somewhere, Guruji?" he innocently asked.

"On a long journey, Sanyal, on a very long journey, my child," I said, knowing how much I was going to miss him.

"Are you going to die?" he asked surprising me with the ease he said it.

"Surya Dada told me when people die they go on a long journey."

I could not hold back my laughter. We continued talking when a little while later Abhedananda arrived. I made Sanyal run along, and we greeted each other as brothers would reuniting after many years.

As the day progressed we made the announcement and necessary arrangements were being made for my departure the next day.

The moment finally came and wishing every one goodbye I began my journey toward Paaro. I was so excited about meeting her, being with her, spending my life with her, having children from her. With her thoughts in my mind I soon arrived at Calcutta.

The city had turned quite modern from the last time I had come here. Hailing a tonga I departed for Kali Ghat, my heart racing fast with the excitement of finally seeing her.

As we were reaching, there was a lot of commotion on the streets. "Whats happening?" I asked the tongawala. "I don't know, sir. But let me find out."

Stopping the tonga, the driver got off and went to a passer-by to ask what was happening.

As he finished his conversation, he came running toward me and told me some anti-British protest was taking place and that the police were getting ready for a lathi charge.

"But I must get there," I tried to explain to him.

"Sorry, sir, it is too dangerous to go any further, and I suggest that even you don't go any further," he spoke with genuine concern.

"You don't understand, I have to meet a person there: I have to go," I tried to explain to him in vain.

"Then can you at least wait here for me? I will go there on foot," I tried to reason with him.

"Yes. Yes, that I can do, but for waiting you will have to pay me extra."

"Don't worry, I will pay you what you don't earn in a week," I assured him.

"How far is the temple?" I asked.

"About 1 kilometer in that direction," he replied.

Hurriedly, I started on foot toward the temple. As I was approaching the temple the street was getting more chaotic. Moving against the crowd I now started gaining speed, getting worried about Paaro. As I continued, from a distance I could hear a shrill voice screaming the command to lathi charge. There were three types of people there, the soldiers, the anti-British activists and the common men. The common men were the ones running away and the activists, instead of running, counterattacked the lathi charge. I now started running toward the temple.

As I was about to reach I heard some gunshots and, as the number of gunshots started to increase, I heard that same shrill voice, this time commanding his troops to open fire. The area was become becoming dark with smoke and violent with gunshots. Bodies were falling with bullet wounds and, just then I could see Paaro standing at a distance of about 50 mtr looking scared, not knowing what to do.

"Paaro, Paaro, run away!" I screamed, but with so much noise around it was useless. I ran toward her dodging the blows of the lathis, when I saw her look at me.

"Swami!" she screamed and started running toward me like a lost child finally finding his parents. The scene was like a battleground but I soon stood still holding Paaro in my arms. "Oh my love, I have come, just as I promised," I said, with great relief in my heart. "Swami, I would have waited all my life," she said, holding on to me.

"We need to run, Paaro," I told her.

"Yes, Swami, I know a way from the rear side."

As we started Paaro suddenly shook violently and froze, and her eyes gave a look of shock as if she had just seen a ghost.

"Paaro, what's happened? We have to move out, we need to hurry!" I screamed in all that commotion.

There was no reply as she, after a couple of seconds, collapsed on the ground with her last word, "Swami . . . ."

Falling on my knees next to her I screamed out her name again and again knowing now that she had been shot.

"Somebody please help! Please, somebody please help!" I sat there screaming looking around and in the distance I saw a soldier aiming his rifle at me and before I could react, I felt the sharp pain in my chest. I had been shot. My body became numb as I fell next to Paaro. As my breathing got slower, I could see Sanyal sitting on my lap, asking me, "Guruji, are you going to die?" I could see Paaro dancing in the gardens of the ashram calling out to me to join her. "I am coming my love, I am coming," I called back.

CHAPTER SIX

THE LAST DRIVE

"I am coming my love, I am coming . . ." I was saying when I felt a few light pats on my cheeks.

"Hey wake up, wake up," I heard a voice and as I opened my eyes I saw Yama the lord of death sitting in front of me sipping wine and smiling at me.

"Oh my God!" I said with relief realizing that it was just a dream, feeling my chest to see if there were any bullet wounds.

Getting composed, I asked Yama, "My lord, that was a just a dream."

"Of course it was, as is this moment, if you look at it in the correct manner. Ignorantly, you may call it your life before your previous one, my dear Nikhil, a whole 35 years of it."

"My lord, I am now able to see it all. I have now understood the significance of the life of Man in the physical, astral and the casual worlds. I have truly been able to comprehend the Gayatri, my lord, then why must I have to go back to Earth?"

"Because, though Nikhil, you may have comprehended it, you still need to experience it in terms of a direct perception. That is where, remember, you will have to journey alone, and in that even I cannot be of any help to you," the lord replied.

"But, my lord, how will that journey be? Let me consider for a moment that should I remember everything that you have told me or I discover all this through my own introspection then what will be the next step? I mean, will I meet someone who will say some magic words and I will start my journey? Or will I go into a meditative trance like Lord Buddha did? How, my lord, will I know that my journey has started?"

"Once Man has been able to perceive what I have told you and the relevance of the philosophy of Gayatri, slowly his outlook toward life will start to change. Many get emotional at this stage, but remember, emotions have to get rejected. Many get passionate at this stage, and that too will have to be rejected, as these feelings will only deviate you from the correct path. Such emotions, Nikhil, may elevate you to higher astral worlds but not as a free soul. Once this fact is established one tends to start getting detached: that too will have to be rejected. With such introspection leading one's life, the soul will start to comprehend its true nature. As tools, one may use what I have mentioned, as this is the age of Kali, and comprehension alone may not suffice. As the days pass the lotus in you will start blooming or you may call it the rise of the symbolic snake coiled and asleep at the bottom of your spine. On the full blossoming of the 1,000-petalled lotus the bliss of which must also be rejected, on that day, Nikhil, tell mankind there will be a man standing in all his splendor, *The Free Soul.* The Greatest of the Greatest, Mightier that the Mightiest, the Lord of the Lords, Lord Vishnu himself."

"But, my lord, you did mention Vishnu was also illusionary and, therefore, also subject to destruction as the highest truth is the dark energy. Then do tell me, my lord, is reaching the abode of Vishnu the highest truth or, reaching the abode of the dark energy the highest truth?"

Smiling, lord Yama continued:

Without a doubt, my dear child, it is the dark energy which is the highest truth. It is from that which everything was created. That is why it is also called the mother of creation. However, know this, that the dark and light energies are interdependent, like you are awake and you are asleep, like there is night and day. Right now the Creator is in a dream state, that's why the glorious light came into being as Vishnu, who is full, the knower of all, knowing whom nothing more needs to be known, with pure bliss, with qualities as mentioned in the scriptures: divine wisdom, power, strength, wealth, fame and dispassion, eternal and infinite, thus giving the formless attributes of the dark energy a form. While we are in the manifested stage it is imperative that we achieve this highest form of existence as that was the cause of the glorious light till such time as the final awakening takes place. At the final awakening the glorious light will dissolve back into darkness. This cycle, my dear child, is ever-continuous.

With these words Yama held my hands and I felt my heart sinking again. I knew the time had come to move on to my next journey. "My lord, don't let me go, please, my lord, I don't want to go back!" I started screaming.

His words echoed in my ears:

I am in the business of death and, I am here to give you company till your next journey that starts in six months Earth time from now. Your soul will be refreshed, as you will be born again and free will, will be your gift. Your experience here will help you and guide you. There will be moments when you will feel the truth—and then in those moments it will be your choice to accept or find the thought foolish and go on with your life in the endless cycle of birth and death as you understand it.

CHAPTER SEVEN

I AM BORN AGAIN

My mind was drowsy with the effects of alcohol and marijuana that made me enjoy the previous night but seemed like a curse this morning. I tried to focus and recollect the previous night just when I found Natasha lying next to me. I cursed myself and hoped I had not got her pregnant. But, by lord, what a body she had! I threw the covers off her to get a good look at her, which gave me some relief from the heaviness in my head.

I got up and headed for the kitchen to get some aspirin. It was 11 a.m. and I knew I had to catch a flight that day at 5. I needed to be in Delhi that night for a meeting with some of my associates.

I was 28 and already the business world had started taking me as a serious player in the market. As I went back to bed, Natasha stirred and snuggled next to me. I felt the urge, and feeling her flesh, we made love once again.

Both of us knew that our relationship was purely physical. I took care of her finances and she took care of me, whenever I was in Mumbai. I really did not have the time to get entangled in relationships and all the complications that accompanied them. Perhaps when the time would be right I would think about settling down. But right now that was the last thing on my mind.

As the aircraft taxied on to the runway for take-off the Boeing's engines roared mightily in splendor, shaking the aircraft as it moved forward finally lifting itself toward the clouds and settling into a cruise at 35,000 ft above the chaotic planet. Sitting next to me was a monk in saffron.

Strangely, it felt peaceful sitting next to him and it made my mind relax, taking my thoughts away from the complex situations that I faced every day.

The aircraft touched down at Delhi and I headed straight for the hotel, where the meeting was scheduled. After the meeting we had a party. It was 11 p.m. I rolled my joint and enjoyed the numbness of my mind that gave me a feeling of being in heaven. To be senseless to the worries of life, according to me, was heaven, and marijuana was the angel that never failed to take me there.

Feeling the high, I met Nisha, who was introduced to me by one of my associates. She was quite attractive and smart too. Having graduated from the London School of Economics she was pursuing her Ph.D. in Hindu philosophy.

I found that quite strange; however, the only thing I was interested in was to know how it would feel to have her naked riding on top of me.

With a bit of chit-chatting I offered her a drink and tried to have a conversation with her on Hindu philosophy, of which I knew nothing. I tried to woo her by telling her that I was a very religious person and that I went to Mata Vaishno temple once a year which, of course, I never did.

Somewhere, I think she found my statement silly and told me that she was doing her Ph.D. in Hindu Philosophy and not on Hindu gods.

"Whats the difference?" I asked.

"Never mind, Mr. Ankit, don't bother," she replied and excused herself.

Stupid b****, I thought, and moved on to look for someone who would make more sense and be good in bed as well. There were many girls who were there who would throw themselves on me. I picked one and left for my suite. But somewhere Nisha excusing herself from me was annoying me.

Had I said anything wrong? Hindu gods and Hindu philosophy, what's the difference, I wondered.

As the days passed I got more and more entangled in my work. My empire was growing and everything was about acquisitions and balance sheets. The only getaway was my marijuana and women, each of whom I treated as a trophy. The moment I acquired one I went after the next.

I was all of 30 years when I was being awarded the entrepreneur of the year award that I bumped into Nisha.

At first when I looked at her I found it hard to place her. But soon I recollected since there were few in my life who had shunned me, especially with the attitude with which she did.

The moment I found her alone staring into one of the paintings I approached her and whispered into her ears quietly from behind, "Hi, Nisha, how are the gods in heaven doing?" As I said this I found myself intoxicated by her fragrance.

Startled, she turned around, spilling her wine on my shirt.

"Oh my God, I am so sorry," she said, frantically trying to clean the wine off my shirt and then suddenly stopped as if in shock.

"Mr. Ankit," she said as if wondering what I was doing in front of her.

"Well, at least I'm glad you remember me, Nisha," I said, surprising her into wondering how I remembered her from such a long time.

"Who would not remember meeting one of the most eligible bachelors?" she said, smiling at me.

"Well, thank you so much for the compliment, Nisha," I said, almost blushing like a teenager.

"Don't be flattered, Ankit. I must also add that I remember you more so for being a Casanova. Actually that leaves me wondering if you should also get an award for that too."

That really did catch me off guard.

"I'm sorry, but what did you just say?" I replied not knowing how to react.

"You heard me," she said, looking at me defiantly.

"Of course, whatever it is that you think of me is absolutely your prerogative. However, what's concerning me is that your glass is empty because of me, so I insist that I get you a replacement," saying which I signaled to the waiter.

As I handed her over a glass and taking one myself I asked her if she would take a walk with me.

"Well, that's the least I could do for spoiling your shirt."

"You really think me to be one of those non-intellectual types, don't you, Nisha?"

"I'm sorry, but what did I do to give you that impression?" she replied as if really surprised.

"C'mon Nisha, studying the human mind and reactions is what has made me what I am today: I do it all the time."

"Well, in that case, why don't you tell me why is it that you think that way?" she asked, challenging me for a reply.

"Well, for starters a person who does not know the difference between Hindu gods and Hindu philosophy is, according to you, intellectually challenged, I guess."

As I said this she smiled and looked at me, "My god, you don't forget Mr. Ankit, do you?"

"Well, actually I don't, especially a conversation with someone as pretty as you."

This time it was her turn to blush like a teenager. "But really do forgive my ignorance What really is the difference?" I asked her, genuinely wanting to know.

"Well, it's a topic that I am still trying to comprehend," she replied, getting lost in thought and then again getting composed she said, "Why the interest, Mr. Ankit?"

"Nothing really, just inquisitiveness."

"Are you flirting with me?"

"And why not, if it also gives me some insight into something I know nothing about?"

"Have you ever read the Bhagwad Gita?"

"Nope, but I have read comics when I was a kid, heard stories and, of course, watched serials, like perhaps every Indian born in my time, but never really read it. Should I have?"

"Why don't you try?"

"Will that qualify me to take you out for dinner?" I asked

"Hmm, we'll see on that one."

"Can I at least have your number, just in case I get stuck in some particular chapter?"

"You are quite impossible," she said, and exchanging numbers, she excused herself.

While driving back I could only think of her. Perhaps for the first time I was not thinking of wanting to get into bed with someone. Just being in her company was so comforting.

As my thoughts were revolving around her, a sudden jolt shook the car bringing it to a halt. The driver got out and got into an argument with the driver who had hit us from the side. Amidst all the confusion a police jeep approached us and more confusion followed as to who was to blame.

"Ram Singh," I called out to my driver and told him to handle the situation and that I would manage to go back on my own.

As I was walking in search of some public transport I heard the ringing of temple bells. Looking around I saw this huge temple on which was written "ISKCON".

What a coincidence, I thought and intuitively just walked toward it. As I entered the premises I was greeted by a lot of people wishing me "Hare Krishna" to which I replied humbly with the same words.

"Excuse me, sir," I called out to one gentleman and asked him if I could get a copy of the Bhagwad Gita.

"Of course, sir," he said and asked me to follow him, guided me into an office, asked me to have a seat, and then went away returning with some sweets and a glass of water.

"Please sir, do have this *prasad*," he urged, which I politely accepted.

By the time I finished having the *prasad* another disciple entered and handed over a copy of the Bhagwad Gita to the gentleman who had got me, who in turn handed it over to me, wishing me again with "Hare Krishna."

"Thank you, sir," I told him and asked how much I had to pay for it.

"Don't worry about the payment, sir, please accept it as a gift," he said, surprising me.

"Please sir, I insist," I persisted in wanting to make the payment.

"Don't worry, Hare Krishna," saying which he left.

Now that really was a coincidence, I thought, and departed for my house.

As the days passed by I forgot about reading the book but kept reminding myself that I must. At the same time I wanted to meet Nisha but somehow my routine was so busy that invariably I would be stuck somewhere or the other. Finally one day I called Nisha but the response came that the mobile number I was trying to call was not reachable. I religiously called every day for almost a month and finally to my great relief one day the bell rang.

"Mr. Ankit, hi what a pleasant surprise," came the reply.

"Thank God, I was almost wondering if I would ever hear from you."

"And why's that?"

"Well, for one thing, your number has been not reachable for almost a month."

"Aah, is that really how long you have been trying to call me?"

"Frankly, yes."

"Well, did you get stuck in any chapter?"

"Actually, let me admit that I have not even started. But yes, I bought the book the day I met you. Would that at least make me deserve to take you out for dinner?"

"Hmm, I am not too sure about that, Ankit."

"Just dinner, that's a promise."

"OK. How about tomorrow, but just lunch?"

"Great, what time?" I asked, making me excited like a teenager going out on his first date.

We met over at the Taj, and with small talk followed a discussion that would bring about a new chapter in my life of something I could have never imagined.

"How's your research coming around?" I asked out of genuine concern.

"Well, frankly it's like a roller coaster ride, fascinating in every aspect."

"Why don't you tell me more?" I prompted. It was wonderful just to hear her speak.

"The beauty about Hinduism, Ankit, is that unlike many who believe it to be a religion, it is not so, but rather a philosophy on the reality of existence of the soul in various manifested forms."

"Wow, slow down now, explain it in a way I can understand," I replied, feeling a little dazed and hypnotized with her words.

"Have you heard about the Upanishads?" she asked.

"Who hasn't?"

"Good, that's a start. What have you heard?"

"Hmm, it's about the Hindu religion, I guess," I answered, feeling awkward that I really had no clue what it was all about.

"You see," she replied, "that's the tragedy, you talk about being religious but do you know the source of this very religion? The source of the very gods, the purpose of Man's existence, and to those questions, Mr. Ankit, lies the answers in the Upanishads, the nectar of eternal life," she said as if passionately obsessed with the topic.

"Fantastic, enlighten me," I replied, "what then is the purpose of life?"

"You tell me. Ankit, what do you feel is the purpose of your life?"

"Well, I guess I must make money, have a wife, kids, take care of them, be religious I guess, and yeah, I guess that's about it," I replied, looking into her eyes and wondered how it would be to have her as my wife.

"That's it?" she asked.

"Well, I guess, should there be anything else?" I replied looking into her eyes feeling hypnotized by her beauty.

"OK, Ankit, tell me how seriously do you want to know about the philosophy of Hinduism?"

"Damn serious," I replied, wondering what she had in mind.

"Want to go for a drive?" she asked.

"Sure; where to?" I asked, now really wondering what she had up her sleeve.

"To introduce you to the philosophy of Hinduism."

"All, set, ma'am. Your car or mine?" I asked, feeling excited about spending more time with her.

"Mine," she replied.

As we drove to the undisclosed destination in her car, I wondered all the time how it would be to settle down with her, and then the thought of making love to her came to my mind—which was immediately dismissed as I found myself entering a crematorium.

"Hey, hey, hey," I repeated, asking her what she was doing.

"Introducing you, Mr. ankit," she replied, now making me wonder if she was one of those unstable in the mind types.

"Out here?" I mumbled.

As we walked around we saw bodies burning, family members crying. Some were leaving after completing the rites, some were coming. Children were running in ignorance as if this were a picnic spot, being scolded periodically. People were dressed simply and some in fancy clothes flashing their Gucci bags and Rolex watches. The air was a mix of death and expensive perfumes. People were busy making calls, some talking about business issues, some busy in making arrangements, and some talking about how long the whole thing was taking. Some people came in expensive cars and some came who were too poor to have one. There were dead bodies waiting in queue to turn to ashes and then there were the alive ones waiting to get back to work. "Life must go on," I overheard someone saying, perhaps to a relative of the deceased.

And then as if snapping me out of a daze Nisha asked me, "What do you think?"

"What do I think about what?" I replied, not having a clue as to what it was that she was trying to prove.

"Is this the purpose of life? To have a wife, kids, to make money, turn old and die, and after your body is burnt to ashes the people will turn around and go back, saying life must go on?"

It took a while for me to digest what she had just asked me. My head was feeling dizzy as if I had been struck with lightning. On the one hand I was wondering how I got myself dragged into this situation and on the other hand I was too dazed with this aspect of reality that I had never realized or even thought about. My mind was throwing thousands of questions at me to which I had no answers.

The only reply I could give to Nisha's question was if she could take me back home. On the way back we did not speak.

As I got out of the car Nisha held my hands and told me she was sorry if in any way she had upset me.

"Not at all, Nisha; as a matter of fact I must thank you," I replied, feeling warm by her touch. "It's just that I am suddenly not feeling too well. But the lunch is still due," I said, trying to lighten the situation.

"Any time," she replied, hugging me and then driving off.

As I entered my room I called my secretary and asked her to cancel all my appointments and switched off my phone. I just needed time to myself. My head was spinning and as I lay down my eyes rolled up uncontrollably as if trying to converge between the eyebrows. I felt relief as all the thoughts started fading from my mind. I just kept going deeper and deeper. My body started to feel numb. I could feel some tingling sensation at the bottom of my spine. It felt very peaceful. I saw a white light coming and going and then coming again. What was this feeling, I wondered. So peaceful . . . .

When I woke up it was about 8 p.m. and I was feeling refreshed like never before. I switched on my phone and then the calls started flowing.

One by one I answered all, everyone wondering what had happened and where I was.

Well, for one thing I could not tell them the truth. I wondered what they would think had I told them that I had gone on a date to a crematorium. Jeez, what a day, I thought and was pretty sure I wouldn't be meeting Nisha for some time. God, what a waste of a good body. Thinking of bodies, after seeing all the dead ones I needed to focus on the live ones, and the best one I could think of now was Natasha's. But that would only be a week from now when I went to Mumbai. I rolled up my joint, and listening to Dire Straits decided to call up Nidhi.

Nidhi had just finished her college and I had met her at a marriage ceremony. She was all curves and only 21. We both shared a passion for marijuana, sex and our likes in music were common.

As she entered we spent time talking, smoking, listening to music and cuddled up cozily. Her lips were tempting me and as I kissed her she lay down below me inviting me to give her pleasure as she would to me. Making love to her was always so passionate and it took my mind off the experience that I had today with Nisha.

CHAPTER EIGHT

I AM BORN AGAIN

I Meet "The Cheat"

The flight to London was on schedule and sitting next to me was a monk in saffron. He looked familiar, perhaps I remembered vaguely how once before I had a monk sitting next to me in a flight. "Well, I guess they all look the same," I thought.

"How you doing, swamiji?" I greeted him.

"Very well," he replied and continued to read *Newsweek*.

Seeing him I remembered Nisha. It was almost a year since I had met her last, wondering what she might be doing.

"So, you a man of God, sir?" I asked the monk, trying to start a conversation.

"Are we not all children of God?" he replied, not taking his eyes off the magazine.

"Yeah sure, I guess," I said.

In a little while again, I could not resist and so questioned him again, "So whats with the saffron?"

"Well, I like it," he replied.

"No, I mean why do you guys wear saffron?"

"Does it annoy you?"

"No, not at all, sir, but what's the significance?" I continued.

"It's a sign of renunciation."

"Renunciation from what?" I asked

"From the attachments of the world," he replied.

"I don't mean to be rude, sir, but you seem pretty attached to the article on beauty pageants in your magazine," I said with a smirk on my face, just then wondering whether I should have passed that comment at all.

In a voice that had changed, he looked at me for the first time and said, "Do you have a problem?" His face showed no expression with long, flowing hair covering his face partially. His eyes looked all white with no pupils visible almost as if he was a ghost.

The look on his face really gave me a fright as I screamed out in shock.

Just then he started laughing as if after scaring a little child.

The air hostess came running asking if everything was OK.

"Yes, yes, thank you, everything's fine," I replied, saying which she went back.

"Whoa," I said, "you really looked spooky, man!" I said in relief.

"Hi, my name is Swami Abhedananda," he said, stretching his hand out to shake mine.

As I reciprocated, I asked him how he did that eye thing making it look all white.

“Aah, that’s nothing but a yoga technique,” he said bursting into a laugh now and then thinking about how he had scared me.

“Man, are all swamis like you? I mean, aren’t you guys supposed to be the serious types?” I asked, not liking the joke to be on me.

“Why?” he asked.

“Well, you all are men of God, and like that’s supposed to be serious stuff, man.”

“Says who?”

“Well God business is serious business, everyone knows it.”

“Well, I don’t know about the serious side, but surely it is big business today,” he said surprising me with his attitude.

“And I tell you Mr. Ankit, it’s the future of business.”

“Wait a moment, how do you know my name?”

“Aah, magic, I am the swami am I not?”

“Wow, man can you really do all that stuff, like future and past stuff?” I asked, suddenly getting excited about being in his company.

“Sure thing, piece of cake,” he said, snapping his fingers.

“Can you tell something about me?” I eagerly asked.

“OK, what?”

“Anything, I mean just say anything, and if that comes true I’ll become your follower.”

“Aah, Mr. Ankit, I would prefer your dollars rather than your following.”

“Man, you are one greedy swami,” I told him.

"Well, you are greedy too, aren't you? You want information for free without paying for it, so that makes you greedy and stingy."

"OK, fine, tell me, how did you know my name?"

"50 pounds for two answers."

"What two answers?" I asked in surprise.

"Well, first I will tell the secret of how I know your name, and second about your future. Is it a deal?" he said, taking his hands out to shake on it.

"10 pounds and it's a deal."

"Not a penny less than 50."

"OK, deal, now tell me," I said, sounding excited.

"Money first."

"Man, you *are* greedy or what!" I said and taking my wallet out I took 50 pounds but before handing them over I asked, "What if the future you predict does not come true?"

"Money-back guarantee, word of mouth," he said snatching the money from my hands.

"OK, so now tell me."

"The answer to the first question is that, the boarding pass sticking out of your pocket has your name written on it and, your future is that you will be in the city of London in the next four hours."

"What kind of nonsense is that!" I reacted instinctively.

"Well, what's wrong with what I told you, and if you are not in the city of London in the next four hrs you can have your 50 pounds back."

"Ok, jokes over, hand me back my money," I said, feeling annoyed that he had taken me for a ride.

"Sure thing, but tell me was there anything I said that was not part of the deal?"

"What rubbish, I know I will be in the city of London in the next four hrs."

"No you don't, sir: what if the flight gets diverted, it happens all the time, or what if the plane would crash?"

"That's nonsense, just give me my money back."

"No, sir," he replied and went back to reading his magazine.

"Bloody cheat," I said loudly ensuring he heard it.

The rest of the flight we never spoke. But one thing was sure that I would never forget his face. "The Cheat" I nicknamed him in my thoughts.

The city of London always made me alive unlike many who found the weather depressing. But I just loved this country.

I checked into the hotel and to my surprise standing next to me was Nisha also checking in.

"What a surprise!" I said, turning toward her.

"Mr. Ankit! Hi, what brings you here?"

"Business as usual for me."

"Aah, busy man."

"How about you?"

"Research as usual."

"Ph.D. in Hindu philosophy, right?"

"Wrong, that's already done."

"Great! So now that makes you Dr. Nisha."

"Yes, sir, that's me."

"So now what's the research on?" I asked, remembering about the date to the crematorium.

"Actually I am now working with the World Bank, researching on the economic reforms in Europe."

"God, you really sound like a roller coaster ride."

"Why do say that?"

"I mean, there is one extreme of research in Hindu philosophy and the other extreme of research in the economic reforms in Europe: what else can I say.

"Which reminds me," I continued, "you should also do research on fraud swamis."

"Why do say that?"

"Well, I just got ripped off of 50 pounds from one of them."

As I said this she burst into laughter. "The great Ankit Sharma gets ripped off by a swami!" she taunted.

"Yeah, I guess that's me."

Just then I was interrupted by the receptionist who handed over the keys to my room.

"Well, I guess I must leave now, but how about catching up sometime, the lunch is still due."

"That's a promise; what's your room number?" she asked, surprising me.

"7777," I told her, wondering if she would come sometime.

"7777, catch you later," she said as I made my way toward the lift.

I had a busy schedule lined up for my visit to London but would manage to take time out if Nisha were to call me. Somewhere I wished she would. Besides, I was pretty sure she was out of that spooky philosophical stuff that she was into. Research on the economic reforms in Europe: the beauty with the brains. Not bad, I thought.

It was on the second night in London that the telephone in my room rang.

"Hi, Ankit, hope I'm not disturbing you."

It was Nisha on the other side. "Not at all: on the contrary I was just about starting to get bored."

"How about a drink?" she asked, surprising me.

"Sure, why not."

"OK, come over to 4302."

Now this really took me by surprise. "Ten minutes" was all I could say.

When I met her, she was already looking a bit drunk. Guess that would explain the boldness in inviting me over.

"Scotch."

"Sure, make it large. I guess I need some catching up to do."

As we sat making ourselves comfortable, we did some catching up.

With a couple of drinks down I could not but help talking about the incident at the crematorium.

"That was one crazy date that you invited me to," I blurted out, hoping just then that I hadn't.

"Well, that was me then."

"Yeah, I guess, the lady who questions the purpose of life."

"Well, one day we will all ask that question: it's just a matter of time when, but anyways that was the past."

"Yup, the past: here's to the future," I said now feeling quite tipsy.

"One more?" she asked teasingly.

"Sure, why not."

As she handed me the glass she sat down next me, arousing me, making me wonder if she wanted me in bed.

I purposely looked into her eyes and whispered, "God, you *are* beautiful."

"Hmmm, tell me more," she whispered back, running her fingers across my face.

"It's your eyes: they're the most hypnotic thing I have ever set my eyes on."

"Hmm, more."

I did not speak further. I just held her by the waist, and moved toward her lips, teasingly, to see if she would respond.

She closed her eyes and waited.

As I buried my lips sensuously into hers she responded, each of us taking bliss in the moment. Her perfume was making it so much more erotic.

My hands started to unbutton her blouse and felt the softness of her breasts, slowly moving down to kiss them.

Her moaning was getting louder and louder.

Lying on top of her we made love like two obsessed animals.

The next morning when I got up, she was not there but there was a note with a rose lying next to me.

Opening it, there was only one word: "WOW".

I couldn't help smiling. We met every night for the next three days of my stay, and surprisingly each time I wanted to meet her even more. I wondered if I was falling in love with her and with the promise of meeting again I left with a heavy heart.

When I reached India I was scheduled to go to a remote location in Bihar, a place called Chunanagar, to see the location for setting up a manufacturing unit.

Based out of Patna, we left early in the morning. On reaching Chunanagar the weather turned extremely violent. It was 11 a.m., and I suggested that we turn around immediately. The driver advised otherwise and suggested that we take shelter somewhere.

"Damn, does this place have any hotel? It's a bloody village," I said in irritation.

The local contact sitting with us said that the only place we could get shelter was at an ashram about 20 km from there.

The storm was only getting worse so we decided that the best thing would be to go toward the ashram.

The road was really bad making the drive feel like being in a boat in a stormy night. The wiper was a little relief to improve the visibility and I wondered how the driver was managing, driving blindly only by the local contact's intuition of when to go straight or when to turn.

In a little while from then the car came to a halt. The local contact, Abhijeet, told us to wait as he dashed out only to return in a little while later, with men holding up umbrellas.

As we got out we ran toward a housing complex of the ashram, and was quite surprised that everything about the place was quite modern considering the location where it was situated. In a little while the rain stopped and the clouds started to clear revealing a majestic scenery of the ashram leaving me awed by the sheer beauty.

“Mr. Abhijeet, what is this place?” I curiously asked.

“Sir, this is a very holy place, built by Swami Sivananda, and overlooked by the grace of his five disciples.”

“Are they here?” I inquired, hoping I could meet them.

“Oh no, sir, you would have to travel a 100 years back in time to meet them, sir. Today it is being run by the trustees, but sir, I will take you to the holy room.”

With these words he guided me through the gardens into a hut. The floor was of mud and the aroma of incense and flowers was strong and refreshing. Up on the wall were eight portraits. The one on top just had a dot. Below it was that of Goddess Kali. Below that was one of Swami Sivananda, the founder of this ashram, and below him there were five portraits in line of the swami’s disciples. Two portraits caught my eye. One was that of Swami Nachiketa. He seemed to have a striking resemblance with me. And the second one shook me a bit as I recollected, “It’s the cheat,” and of that there was no doubt in my mind. With a little hesitation I asked Abhijeet to tell me about him.

“Sir, he is Swami Abhedananda.”

Hearing the name itself made my feet go cold. That was the same name he had introduced himself with.

“Tell me more, Abhijeet,” I spoke as if still in shock.

"They call him the deathless one, sir, and some call him the time traveler. He took over the ashram after Swami Nachiketa departed for the Himalayas for meditation."

My head was now spinning as I started visualizing scenes coming in flashes before my eyes as if being reflected from a projector.

I saw sitting on the chair ahead of me Swami Nachiketa, with a child on his lap.

"Guruji, why the tears?" the child seemed to be asking.

"My dear child, there is something important that I must tell you," the swami replied.

"What is it, Guruji?"

"There comes a time when a person has to move on, as must I."

"Are you going somewhere, Guruji?" the child asked.

"On a long journey, Sanyal, On a very long journey, my child."

"Are you going to die?"

And then I saw them both laughing.

The scene changed and this time and I saw the same swami making love to a woman he kept calling Paaro.

The scene changed again.

This time I saw the same swami standing in front of another he was referring to as guruji. And then the man spoke.

"Nachiketa, as my body dematerializes all your powers will be gone. You will come strongly under the purview of karma, so be warned of the downfall."

There were many more such flashes of which nothing was making sense. My head was bursting and I don't remember when I passed away.

When I woke up, I found myself in a hospital room with needles stuck in my hands.

The nurse came running toward me to check if I was OK. I was feeling absolutely fine, as a matter of fact quite refreshed.

She made a call and in no time a group of doctors entered my room.

"What happened, doctor?" I asked, not being able to recollect how I found myself in this situation.

"Actually nothing, you just fainted, and that too for almost 24 hours. It's nothing to worry about, it must be just stress. You should take some time off," the doctor spoke with concern.

"I will consider that doctor, but can I leave now?"

"Just a few more tests and we will discharge you in a couple of hours."

As the doctor was instructing his team I slowly tried to recollect what had happened.

Then, just like a flash I recollected everything. I was at the ashram and had started seeing flashes of scenes in a projection-like manner. What was that? I kept wondering and thinking whether I should share it with the doctors. But I knew they would attribute it to some sort of stress. This was no ordinary experience that I had just experienced—and also not natural. My meeting with Abhedananda on the flight, my road trip to Chunanagar, the sudden storm, we being driven to the ashram, my striking resemblance with the portrait of one the swamis in the ashram. It was inexplicable and I knew I could not share this with anyone else less they start considering me to be a person with traits of insanity. This could be dangerous for my growing empire, and unnecessary gossip could cause a lot of damage to my reputation. But as I was thinking about all this I was also feeling an intense desire to discuss this with someone. Perhaps I could speak about it to Nisha. She was the only one I could think of who would at least lend me a sympathetic ear. Could this have anything with the past life, I wondered, but rubbished the idea though not with too much conviction. I took a diary and a pen and thought of noting everything that I could remember from that incident.

I noted the date and started penning my thoughts.

Location: Sivananda's Ashram/Chunanagar

Characters seen: Swami Nachiketa/Paaro/Swami Abhedanada/Guruji/ Sanyal.

Swami Nachiketa sitting with a child referring to him as Sanyal. The swami was talking about going somewhere far. The child asked him if he was going to die. Then there was laughter.

Swami Nachiketa making love passionately with a girl he was referring to as Paaro

A person Swami Nachiketa was referring to as guruji who was warning Nachiketa to be careful as he was going to come strongly under the purview of karma.

Swami Nachiketa was holding Swami Abhedananda in his arms and wishing each other goodbye.

Swami Nachiketa was instructing a man on the specifications on the making of an idol of Goddess Durga.

That's about it, I thought. There were many more scenes but I could not seem to recollect them in detail. I carefully kept the diary and was now looking forward to meeting Nisha, hoping she would be able to throw some light on the incident.

After I was discharged I was quite distracted by my work the next couple of days. The incident at the ashram was nagging me as I was desperately seeking for some answers. I called up Nisha, but told her nothing about the incident as I did not want to discuss it over the phone, however, did find out that she would be here in about a month's time. That is how much I would have to wait before I shared it with her.

The incident had now changed my perspective toward life. The journey to the crematorium with Nisha now started to make sense and, for the first time I questioned myself as to what my purpose in life was. Why was I born and where do we go after death and with these thoughts I picked up the Bhagwad Gita and started to read hoping I would get some answers to my questions.

CHAPTER NINE

I AM BORN AGAIN

The Quest

As the days passed, I got more and more engrossed in reading the Gita. It was fascinating and I wondered why I had deprived myself of such a wonderful gift to mankind. However, needless to add I did not get the answers to what I was seeking. Somewhere the answers were not convincing me enough.

As Arjun bowing down before the great army of the Kauravas at Kurukshetra and then being instructed by Lord Krishna on the truth and reality of life, I related myself with Arjun. However, in my existence Lord Krishna was missing. I started visiting spiritual gurus and each of them had words of wisdom to offer, however, I was still not convinced. I knew if any of them had convinced me then I would not be feeling the emptiness that I was.

The level of frustration was growing. On the one hand I was handling an empire that was growing at a phenomenal rate and on the other hand here I was seeking something entirely different.

The most common guidance I got from all the spiritual gurus that I met was to give up everything and fall at the feet of the Lord.

But why should that be, I would question. The answers invariably would be because everything was an illusion.

Perhaps, I would often introspect but, not with conviction. I remembered once Nisha talking about the Upanishads and the Vedas referring to them as the nectar of eternal life and so I made the effort to read them as well but could not grasp any of what was written. Someone advised me to read the Brahma sutras but reading that too was beyond me.

I cannot say that I had turned spiritual, since I believe it is a strong word to describe anyone and as far as I was concerned I was still indulging in everything that defies spirituality.

I had my women, sex and indulgence in marijuana, and so kept wondering why these thoughts were bothering me so much.

It was difficult to take time out to visit spiritual gurus but I would try and do so as often as I could. I wondered what people saw in them to blindly become their followers giving up everything in their lives. Many of the disciples were highly successful and even educated people with degrees from institutes of great repute. They had sacrificed everything to come under the grace of these men who claimed to be enlightened gurus, each one claiming the other was a fraud, but their answers did not seem to convince me. One of the disciples I met even told me that I was not getting the answers to my questions because I was too attached to worldly illusions.

"So what must I do?" I asked.

"Give up everything," he answered.

"Easier said than done, sir, but do convince me why."

"Because the world is an illusion."

"How do you know that? I could say that *you* are under an illusion to have given up everything and fallen under the spell of this man who calls himself a swami and travels the world in his private jet and owns I don't know how many luxury cars."

"Oh, child, you are under the spell of maya, and so you don't see," he continued.

"So show me," I challenged him.

"For that you must have the grace of a guru."

"And do you feel, sir, that you have the grace of the guru?"

"But of course, my child, he is kind and guides us in our journey toward freedom."

"Aah, so that's his promise: freedom, is it?"

"Yes, my child, that's why we are all here."

"Why are we all here, sir?"

"To get freedom from the clutches of maya."

"And can you show me, sir, anyone who has got this freedom?"

"That would be Guruji, my child."

"How do know, sir, that anything called freedom exists? That could also be an illusionary thought."

"For that, one will have to feel."

"Feel what?"

"Peace."

"So tell me, sir, are you seeking peace or, are you seeking freedom?"

"Freedom is peace, my child."

"Can you stop calling me child? My name is Ankit."

"Very well, ankit, you may stop calling me sir, my name is James."

"From where?" I asked, enjoying the discussion that I was having.

"California."

"So tell me, James, why did you leave everything and become Guruji's disciple?"

"To seek peace."

"Peace from what?"

"Peace from the problems of life. There is sadness everywhere and, Guruji offers us peace. To serve him is peace."

"You mean freedom."

"No, Ankit, for that we must wait for the grace of Guruji."

"So, James, are you seeking peace or freedom?"

"Peace is the path that will lead to freedom."

"And what happens when one achieves freedom?"

"Then one becomes one with the Lord."

"You mean there is something called God that exists?"

"But of course."

"How can you be so sure?"

"Because one can feel him."

"Let me ask you, James, according to you all that exists is an illusion, right?"

"absolutely."

"Then everything that we think or feel is also an illusion, and if that is true then tell me if you feel the presence of the Lord then that is also an illusionary thought."

Abruptly James got up and said, "I must leave now, Ankit. I can only pray that may the Lord be kind and show you the path."

"Very well, James, I'll pray for that too," saying which we parted ways.

I was amazed as to how and why I was asking these questions. I was in no way trying to put James down and neither trying to prove one-upmanship with him. I was just seeking answers and came to two fundamental conclusions that would help me in my quest on this journey.

The first was: One must not have blind faith. The reason was that I realized a lot of these disciples were in a mode of escapism from hectic lives and with sweet words of fake swamis they get lured into a greater illusion of seeking freedom from what even they do not know in the true sense of spirituality.

The second was: Question everything till it is conclusively proven.

The reason I came to the second conclusion was that in many encounters I was told that it is right because it is so mentioned in the scriptures.

However, surely after questioning and introspecting everything if one will realize that what is written in the scriptures is true as revealed to the seeker then only may that man be worthy of preaching the scriptures should he choose to instead of someone saying "because it is so mentioned." The point to understand is *why* was it so written.

As the days passed, Nisha never came and everytime her trip got postponed for some reason or the other.

In the meantime I tried to find out everything about the ashram and the disciples of Sivanada but there was little that could help in explaining that incident. In one of the parties I was attending someone was talking about past life regression wherein one can experience his or her past life. I was tempted but controlled myself less I start indulging in too much of all this stuff that could lead me getting into an obsessive mode, not that to some extent I already believed that I had.

It was on one of my business trips to Kolkata that an important client insisted that I accompany him to a temple called Dakshineshwar. It was here that I also visited a room where Swami Ramakrishna resided. He was a great saint, as Dr. Sen, our client, was educating me.

"I really didn't know that you were the spiritual type, doc."

"Oh, not really, but one must live a balanced life and thank the Almighty for the kindness she bestows upon her children."

I wanted to get into a discussion mode with him, but thought otherwise in case he misunderstood my motive.

Now this was really becoming a problem. If I questioned anyone they would think of me as being an atheist wherein my purpose was never that. Needless to add, the few friends that I secretly made in the so-called 'spiritual' circle had now started avoiding me. Not that it mattered to me but, the answers were just not coming.

"Do you know, Ankit, five years back I was given up for dead with a disease that had no cure?" Dr. Sen said, interrupting my thoughts.

"What happened?"

"A rare cancer, and it was then that I was blessed by a guru and miraculously I stand before you today."

"C'mon doc, don't tell me you believe in all this."

"Frankly, Ankit, neither did I, especially being a medical practitioner myself, but life is more than what meets the eye."

"Who is this man? Can I meet him?"

"Why not? But I cannot come with you, I'm afraid."

"Why, he's the man who saved your life didn't he?"

"True, but such was his condition. You see, he was my father's guru. My father died when I was only a child, but he had introduced my mother to him. My mother used to visit him religiously whenever time permitted. When my disease was diagnosed she went to him for help. He turned her away saying that was my destiny. My mother had full faith in him and said she would starve to death if he didn't help me. How can a mother bear the loss of her husband and her only child? The guru told her he would help if she promised never to visit him again. I myself have met him only once. While I was lying in bed he entered the room with my mother. He asked her to leave and with his stick he tapped me on my head thrice and made me promise that I would visit Dakshineshwar Temple once a year to thank Goddess Kali for her kindness in recovering me."

"That's it?" I said in awe.

"That's it," replied Dr. Sen.

Had anyone else related this story I would have laughed out loud. But coming from the doc there was no doubt in my mind, making me excited that this may just be the man who could give me the answers which I sought.

"How soon can I meet him, doc?"

"Well, if you want, today itself. He stays around 30 kilometers from here."

"Doctor, if you don't mind can I take your leave to go and meet him?"

"What is it, Ankit? Don't tell me you have some incurable disease."

"Nothing like that, doc, just some unanswered questions."

Writing the address in a note pad and instructing the driver with directions we parted ways with the promise of catching up for dinner later in the evening.

The drive took longer than I had anticipated. The road was rough and muddy. On reaching the destination we had to ask for some directions to Swamiji's house. Everyone seemed to know him well. On reaching the house, which was bigger than I had imagined, the door was opened even before I knocked. Perhaps it was the sound of the car, not many of which I had seen around here.

It was an old lady who had opened the door asking me what I wanted.

"I would like to meet Swamiji," I replied.

"Swamiji is meditating; sit inside, I will inform him," saying which she seated me comfortably and went to call the swami.

I was wondering how I would greet him, and what questions would I ask. Now suddenly I was stuck with the thought of how I should frame my questions. Would it sound too ridiculous to just ask him what was the purpose of life? Or why we are born? A doubt entered my mind making me wonder if it was a rash decision I had taken on the spur of the moment to come here. I wondered how I would start and if he would give the same advice that many others had given. As these thoughts were storming my mind I felt a tap on my shoulder. Turning around in fright, I saw a man perhaps in his 60s staring into my eyes. I got up instinctively but he forcefully made me sit.

Coming around now in front of me he stood staring into me.

I was at a loss for words, not knowing how to react.

"OK, now you may stand up," he commanded.

As I stood up with his hands he started to probe my face like a doctor would to a patient.

"How have you been?" he asked.

"Fine, Swamiji," I replied, not knowing how to further the discussion.

"Good, now you follow me, the time has come," he said and started to walk.

Without bothering to question him I submissively followed him. He led me to a small empty room and asked me to sit.

With a little trouble and adjustments I managed to sit on the floor with my legs folded like one sees the saints sitting. Seeing me struggle he laughed as if in disbelief.

"Now listen to me carefully," he spoke, suddenly becoming serious.

"I am going to induct you into Kriya Yoga."

"What's that?" I asked inquisitively.

"Just some simple breathing exercise."

"But why do you want to?"

"It is *you* who are seeking the answers, are you not?"

"Yes, but how do you know what answers I am seeking?" I replied, realizing that whoever he was, he was obviously some advanced yogi.

"Why don't you focus on the serious questions, instead of wasting your time on the silly ones?" he replied almost as if he was reprimanding me.

I spoke no more. For the next half an hour he taught me some simple exercises.

"If you are seeking the answers, then ensure that you spend as much time in practicing what I have taught you." Saying these words he then told me that I could leave.

"That's it?" I replied.

"That's it," he answered.

"But I don't understand what is the purpose of doing this."

"You ask too many questions."

"Should I not?"

"Of course, but ask yourself—and then the answers will be revealed to you."

"Why can't someone not just tell me, like for example why can't you?"

"Because the journey has to be your own."

"But do tell me, what is the purpose of this initiation into Kriya?"

"Very well, then listen and understand whatever little bit that you can. When one is initiated into Kriya by an apt person, then it is like someone putting a switch into the on position. Now that the switch is on, it does not necessarily mean that there will be light. For the light to come there must be presence of electricity. The practice of Kriya generates that electricity, and one needs to produce it in plenty for the light to shine brightly in our minds, thus revealing the truth of life. Do you now understand?"

"Yes, I now understand the significance," I replied, feeling satisfied as to *why* I must do Kriya instead of blindly doing it just because someone has asked me to.

"Guruji, can you tell me tell me about the purpose of life?"

"What's there in telling you about the purpose of life? Do what you are doing, enjoy what you are doing, now run along and I shall meet you soon."

"You will meet me again?" I spoke in surprise.

"Yes, when the time comes."

"But, Guruji, I am a very busy man and I travel a lot, so why don't you tell me when and accordingly I will come?"

"Go now," he said as if getting rid of a student who was pestering his teacher too much.

I touched his feet and started my drive back toward Kolkata realizing for the first time that it was almost as if the swami had been expecting me.

In the past few years since my visit to the crematorium it was only today that I felt that I was in the presence of a man who had all the answers to my questions. I was excited about practicing the Kriya technique and even more about meeting this man everyone called Swamiji again.

I recollected from the many scriptures that I had read that when the time was right the guru would manifest himself in front of the disciple, leaving me to think whether in my life he was the one.

I met Dr. Sen at a club in the evening and over a couple of drinks shared my strange experience with him.

"I don't know how to thank you enough, Doc," I said with genuine gratitude for having given me the opportunity to have met such a great saint.

In—my hectic schedule I tried to take as much time as I could to practice Kriya Yoga. I knew something was transforming within me. It was not as if I was becoming detached toward my business or my indulgences but, somewhere by doing Kriya I was becoming more introspective. The answers to my questions were being revealed to me one by one. I would not allow myself to be satisfied by any one particular answer lest it be a manifested thought, misguiding me instead of doing otherwise. It was a wonderful journey in my life wherein it felt like a game of hide and seek. It was the Lord who was hiding and I was the seeker. "Find me if you can," I nicknamed these moments of introspection.

When I finally met up with Nisha and shared all my experiences with her, she stared into my eyes in disbelief.

"You have changed, Ankit."

"For the better or the worse?" I asked teasingly.

"That I will tell you a little later," she said, and kissing me, started to unbutton my shirt as I sensuously undid hers.

We made love passionately and when exhausted she lay down next to me and breathing heavily she said, "For the better."

We held each other, making me wonder if it was time for me to settle down and start a family.

I thought of proposing to her, but restrained myself thinking it might be a little too early. Besides, I doubted whether she would be ready for it. She seemed to have drawn out her career path and seemed to be quite aggressively involved.

After a week of having a great time with Nisha, she departed for London making me go back to focus on my daily affairs of work and practicing Kriya which I had totally forgotten about during her stay.

It was during one of my meditations that I experienced a strange encounter. I was close to 10 minutes into the practice of meditation that I felt as if I was getting sucked into something. I got so frightened that I snapped out of my practice. I got up and lit a cigarette and wondered what that was and why had I got so scared. It could have been a unique experience that I had deprived myself of. Gathering courage, I decided to attempt once more. I once again sat down and again in about 10 minutes that same feeling came. I was scared again but decided to wait a little more. The feeling was as if I was getting pulled into a wormhole. There was a tremendous tingling sensation at the bottom of my spine and the speed of being pulled was getting stronger. Now I was really scared and wondered whether I should snap out but once again thought to wait for some more time. In a little while from then the pulling sensation stopped. I had lost my sensation of the body and it was as if I was just the mind itself. The feeling was peaceful. Just then the pull started again but, there was no pain and no fear. My mind was enjoying it like a child would on a roller coaster ride. I cannot recollect what happened after that. I had gone blank. Slowly, in some time I started to feel the sensation of my mind with thoughts of peace, a different peace that cannot be explained. Then I started to gain consciousness of my body. First, as if it was in a distance, and then slowly becoming a part of it, limiting the vastness of my mind into the confines of my body which felt small and insignificant.

As a matter of fact when I opened my eyes everything felt small. My existence, my business empire, my acquisitions, this entire planet and life itself felt insignificant. It was a strange experience and the detachment lasted for almost an hour after which everything started to become normal. I switched on my phone and the calls started coming. As I got entangled in the daily affairs that feeling of peace had vanished making me now hungry for more. Slowly and steadily my outlook toward life started to change. For one thing I did stop womanizing and thought of it as a great sin that I had been doing. It was not as if I chose to become a *brahmachari*, but surely I wanted now to settle down and have a stable life.

When I met Nisha the next time I proposed marriage to her, which she declined, and that was the last I ever saw of her. I had always thought that whoever I proposed to would jump at the opportunity, that was how arrogant and proud I was. It was my delusion that got shattered with Nisha and I can only thank her for that.

I was now in a stage of depression neglecting my work and spending more and more time in meditation. The business had started to suffer but I stopped caring about it. I had delegated the work to people I trusted but somehow I found myself lacking in judgment of their efficiency. This reaction was in no way related with Nisha but rather a dejection in finding this life meaningless. My meditation sessions were getting longer and when disturbed I would curse the people thinking them to be devils in disguise.

But now all my answers were being cleared one by one. I started to feel proud about my knowledge and looked down upon people thinking them to be inferior because of lacking in spiritual insight.

To justify my answers I started to read the ancient scriptures to see if there was any contradiction in what I had perceived intuitively with what was written in them.

I started with the Bhagwad Gita, and this time believed that I had grasped everything that was written. I attempted the Vedas, the Upanishads and could fully comprehend what was written. With the commentaries on Brahma Sutras I understood exactly what Adi Sankaracharya was trying to preach. It was almost shocking how everything that I had perceived was also what was written in the scriptures. This only boosted my ego to higher levels.

But one thing was bothering me. How come it was that people with great knowledge also had great spiritual abilities like travelling in time, manifesting themselves anywhere, travelling through multidimensional worlds, etc. and how it would be possible for me to achieve those powers. With the knowledge I had got I thought it was only right that I should also deserve these powers. I felt I must visit Guruji who had initiated me in Kriya and ask him for guidance. He had promised to meet me but already two years had passed so I decided that I should pay him a visit.

I called up my secretary and asked her to book me a flight to Kolkata and make the necessary arrangements.

That evening Rajesh, a long-time friend and the CEO of my company came to visit me.

Over a couple of drinks and a joint of marijuana neither of which I had left indulging in, he picked up the topic I was hoping he wouldn't. It was about the losses the company was suffering.

"At this rate, Ankit, we will have start thinking of downsizing," he spoke with genuine concern.

"Why, what's the problem? There are always ups and downs in life, Rajesh: what is up today will be down tomorrow and what is down today will be up tomorrow," I replied with a dash of philosophy.

"What's gotten into you, Ankit? You were never like this."

"And what was I like, just another ignorant fool?"

"For godsake, Ankit, stop it. You have started talking like a recluse and people are gossiping thinking that it has something to do with drugs."

"The world may call me mad and such is the way I think of them," I said, slurring, perhaps having had too much to drink.

"For god sake, Ankit, the business needs you!"

"The business has you, why the hell can't you handle the situations, don't you think you are f****** good enough, you are the f****** CEO for godsake and if you can't f****** handle it then tell me I will hire a guy who can. But stop f****** crying in front of me like a f****** cry baby!" I reacted screaming at Rajesh for the first time ever.

"What the f*** do you mean?" This time Rajesh raised his voice.

"You bloody well know what I f****** mean, you good for nothing loser."

"Who's calling who a loser, you a******? Everyone knows that you are nothing but a skirt-chasing drug addict."

"Oh yes, Oh yes, that's me alright Don't forget I am the guy who build the goddamn empire that f****** pays your salary."

"F*** your salary and f*** your job, Ankit, nobody wants to be a part of a drowning ship."

"There goes the f****** stinky rat as the ship sinks. But don't forget I am the captain and I will set sail again, you bloody good-for-nothing CEO. Chief Executing Zero." Having said this I couldn't help but start laughing with my new-found interpretation of CEO.

"Rajesh the CEO, the Chief Executing Zero," I continued laughing as Rajesh smashed his glass on the floor and walked out.

The next day I was not ashamed of anything that had transpired between me and Rajesh. He was actually doing a rotten job and was too dependent on me for taking decisions. I would have sacked him a long time ago had it not been for our friendship and with me being involved, the CEO was more so just a signing authority for me.

Although I was getting detached from my business I did not entirely want to let it slip out of my hands. I was not ready yet to sacrifice everything.

I cancelled my trip to Kolkata for sometime and decided to focus on my business and revive it hoping I would find someone efficient to handle it.

The next six months passed by with me now once more involved in my business. It was almost as if I was leading the life of someone with a split personality. On the one had I was the businessman and on the other a seeker. It seemed as if there was an ongoing battle between the flesh and soul. I was reminded of the battle of Kurukshetra and now believed that perhaps it was apt to say that such was the truth of life, where one is Arjun who is battling not a war with weapons but a battle between the flesh and the soul. Who reigns supreme is the destiny of every individual.

I read the Gita again and found a new meaning of how to interpret it. As time passed I found a new CEO. Her name was Jyoti, and perhaps the most efficient person I had met, a women I admired and respected and had full faith in.

I was confident that she could steer the company in the right direction and, as time would tell, she did.

I now felt I could spend more time in meditation and had drastically cut down on my consumption of marijuana, but my intake of alcohol was increasing.

I once again made arrangements for my travel to Kolkata to meet the swami. However, on reaching his house I was told that he had left on a journey and no one could say exactly when he would return. It could be six hours, six days or maybe even six months.

I got frustrated at hearing what I did—and started to wonder and introspect why. The answers came simply. An action has a reaction.

“But why?” I tried to introspect once again asking myself.

The answer echoed in my ear, "Such is the truth."

"What truth?" I questioned myself in frustration.

"If there is desire, there is disappointment, like a see-saw."

The words sounded familiar as if I had heard them somewhere or someone had mentioned them before. Was I going in the right direction, I wondered? Was there actually any truth in anything called spirituality or were the modern-day scientists correct in rejecting the whole concept? No, that could not possibly be, I convinced myself. There had to be greater purpose in life rather than a freak accident and attribute it only to the Big Bang theory.

I started focusing on my Kriya practice knowing somewhere that my approach was wrong, not where the Kriya was concerned, but toward my thought process. I felt strongly the desire to have a guru but somehow did not get that feeling of total surrender with anyone who claimed to be one.

It was in Rishikesh where we had gone for an office outing that I finally met the swami who had inducted me into Kriya. Seeing him I fell at his feet.

He held my hands and as if telepathically the words echoed in my ears.

"As a disciple if you are desperately seeking a teacher, then rest assured there is a teacher even more desperately seeking you. When the time is right it is the guru who seeks out the disciple and not the other way around. And also understand, the guru need not be in physical form. He could be from a high astral planet: you just need to tune in because he has already tuned into you. Otherwise you would have not asked the thought-provoking questions in the first place."

As the words finished, the swami smiled at me, and embracing me, vanished into thin air.

It took me some time to figure out whether the incident was a hallucination or the truth and believed with my whole heart that yes, it was the truth. With this little incident I believed even more strongly that I was on the right path and I felt a change come within me.

CHAPTER TEN

I AM BORN AGAIN

The Transformation

In the past couple of years since I had started my practice of Kriya there was no doubt in my mind that I was progressing at an extremely rapid pace. But having had said that, I also realized that it was also accompanied by extreme mood swings. There was a phase in my life when I underwent extreme depression and frustration. Then came another phase where I found the very purpose of life meaningless, making me almost live the life of a recluse. I bounced back only to be engulfed with an ego that made me feel proud of my knowledge and look down upon people for their lack of spiritual insight. But now a new sort of transformation was developing within me. In my moments of meditation I felt the radiance of light coming from an unseen source through which the cosmic play of life was being exhibited. The concept of the illusionary world was now more clear in my mind than ever. Within us was dwelling the Lord and, we were all his reflections. This made me feel that if such was the truth then everything around us is the Lord.

I cursed myself for my past actions and for all the sins I had committed. I gave up all my addictions and used my money for building temples and organizing satsangs. I was getting so passionate that I would spend hours crying out to the Lord to have mercy on me and bless me with His grace. At times I would get so passionate that my body would start to convulse.

In everything that I saw, I saw the Lord, be it in men, women, children, animals, plants and anything else that there was. How beautiful life was. I had entirely washed my hands off business but Jyoti my CEO insisted that I hold on.

"Look at how many people have employment because of you, be it directly or indirectly," she would invariably remind me.

I gave in to her arguments and handed her over my power of attorney. While she was making the money I was spending it wherever I felt I could make a difference to mankind. The arrangement was just fine by me.

I would spend much time in travelling and meeting spiritual people with or without fame. Those whom I would once look down upon I started respecting for what they spoke, be it the truth or of words coming from a vulture dressed in saffron. Forgiveness was the key nature of the merciful Lord and as His humble servant one must do as He does. Pride vanished from my heart and everything I did was as if on the instructions of the Almighty.

My passion was increasing day by day and I now chose to stay in a temple I had built with humble surroundings doing the cleaning and washing myself.

In my mind there was nothing but the light of the Almighty.

People had now started calling me swamiji, and as much I would insist not to refer to me by that name they would not have it any other way.

It was on a stormy night while sleeping when one of the devotees of the temple came to me saying that there was a gentleman whose car had broken down and requested shelter in the temple. The temple that I had built was quite a distance from the city and sparsely populated.

"Send him in," I told Ajay and got up to make some arrangements so that I could accommodate the guest comfortably. The lights had gone off and lighting a candle I went to welcome the guest.

"Please, sir, do come in."

"Thank you so much, sir, the driver has gone looking for help and I shall leave as soon as he comes."

I tried to convince him that there was no inconvenience and that he could stay for as long as he wished.

"So are you the head priest of this temple?" he asked trying to start a conversation.

"No, sir, no one is a head here; all of us are in the service of the Lord," I replied.

I could not see his face clearly as it was dark and his hair drenched with rain was all over his face.

Making him sit comfortably I asked ajay to make tea for the guest.

"You speak excellent English, sir, obviously you are educated, then how come you are out here? I mean, I don't mean any disrespect, but are you one of those who has sacrificed everything and taken to spirituality?" he asked, sounding genuinely confused with my presence out here.

"Don't spiritual people speak English?"

"No, sir, I didn't mean that, but in such a remote location like this, one usually doesn't come across them."

"Oh, my dear friend, my education is of little significance to the qualified men I have met who are great souls. I am of little consequence in their presence."

"But tell me, sir, why do you do this?"

"Do what?" I replied, not being able to understand the point he was getting across.

"I mean, sacrifice everything and escape from worldly life."

"What makes you think I am escaping?"

"I don't mean to offend, sir, but God created this world to live and enjoy, then why abandon it and live a life of a medicant?"

"Who says I have abandoned everything? I have just dedicated my life to serve the Lord."

"But, sir, surely the Lord who has created everything does not require your services. Of what possible service could you possibly be doing for him?"

I was a little taken aback by this statement and somehow was reminded of myself many years ago. It was almost as if it was another life. But I knew I must guide him and forgive his ignorance.

"I try to spread his teachings to those who have lost direction in life."

"From this temple out here in the wilderness?"

"Well, I am not always here; I do whatever I can that is in my ability."

"Then why do you come here?"

"Because it is peaceful and I can serve the Lord."

"So, sir, you come here for peace or to serve the lord?"

"In serving the lord I get peace."

This was so much happening like a discussion I remembered having with one the disciples of a self-proclaimed guru that I had met and knew that I must convince this man to understand the truth.

"One must understand that we are all a reflection of the Lord in an illusionary world which we, because of ignorance, accept as truth. To overcome this ignorance one must fall at the feet of the Lord so that He may be merciful in guiding us."

"So, sir, tell me, would one get the Almighty's grace only if he sacrifices everything and wears saffron? If we are all children of God then why the discrimination?" he continued adamantly.

"The Lord does not discriminate, my friend, He waits patiently for anyone who cries out to Him, always there to help."

"Help what?"

"Help the ignorant soul to understand his true nature."

"Which is what, sir?"

"The true nature of every soul is that of the Lord."

"So what is his nature?"

"He is the final truth knowing whom nothing more needs to be known."

"So, sir, one on the spiritual path is seeking peace and to become one with the Lord?"

"That is true, my friend."

"Tell me, sir, I am a businessman. I seek money and you seek peace; I seek fame and you seek the Lord; both of us are seekers, then where is the difference?"

"The difference lies in the fact that I seek the truth and you after illusionary aspects of life."

"I stand here in the flesh, sir, as you in front of me. What seems my illusion, sir, is also yours. We both seem to be here in the moment, you no different from me."

"The difference, my friend, lies in the perception of discriminating between real and what's unreal and there lies the difference between you and me."

"The truth as I see, sir, is that we are both seekers: I tread my path as you do yours. Somewhere, I perceive, sir, that true spirituality is when one stops seeking, otherwise how are you any different from me?"

Before we could further our discussion the gentleman's driver came saying that the car had started and that they could continue with their journey.

We wished each other goodbye and parted ways.

Somewhere the gentleman's last comment had started to bother me, "True spirituality is when one stops seeking."

I wondered who this man was. I had forgotten to even ask his name or even got a good look at his face due to there being no electricity but, surely whoever he was he had got me thinking.

I called ajay and asked him if the man had introduced himself to him.

"Yes, Swamiji, before he was getting into the car he told me to tell you his name, but I forgot. It was a funny name."

"Think, Ajay, what was it?"

"Yes, Swamiji, I remember now: he said to tell you he was the cheat."

What kind of funny name is that, but before I could think further I froze. What ajay was trying to tell me was that before the gentleman was leaving he told him to tell me that he was "The Cheat," none other than Swami Abhedananda, the swami I had met on the flight and nicknamed "The Cheat," whose portrait I had seen in the ashram. "The deathless one, the time traveler," I recollected Abhijeet having told me.

CHAPTER ELEVEN

I AM BORN AGAIN

The Rise of the Snake

There was no doubt in my mind that there was a higher intervention in my life for it to have taken a turn in a manner in which it did. My point of contention was what was it that was expected of me. In the past few years my journey in search of the truth and finding a meaningful purpose to life had once again brought me to a point of introspection on whether this passion within me and my love for the Almighty was the final answer to Man's existence. I would have thought so until my last encounter with Abhedananda. What did he mean by, "True spirituality is when one stops seeking"? Somewhere, perhaps, I realized that had these words been spoken by someone else I would have discarded them as coming from an ignorant soul. This also made me realize that there was still in me a sense of pride for trying to claim to know everything. But my perspective now took a different turn. There was no physical presence of a guru in my life, but I was confident that someone was watching and guiding me. I now started reading the Brahma Sutras and focusing on the Advaita Vedanta philosophy of life. Now one must understand what Advaita Vedanta is. In this philosophy as revived by Adi Sankaracharya he proclaimed that only Brahman is real, the only truth, and the rest is all unreal. Having said this he justified that there was also no difference between the Brahman (do not mistake Brahman with Brahma of the Holy Trinity) and the individual self.

On further introspection I realized that if Brahman was the only truth and everything else was unreal, then every feeling that we had, every desire that we felt was also illusionary, be it of love for God or love for money, hate, desire or any thought since it was only a projection of the supreme mind. But if this was the case then what was the purpose of creation or this projection at all, I questioned myself. I was also left wondering as to why a preacher of Advaita Vedanta wrote the famous song called "Bhaja Govindum" where he praises Lord Vishnu and reiterates the importance of falling at the feet of Lord Vishnu as he is the only truth and our only savior. There seemed to be a sort of contradiction. As Advaita Vedanta speaks of only the Brahman (The Formless) to be real and the rest all unreal, by that understanding Lord Vishnu would also be unreal. So why would a man like Sankara so passionately write such words to tell mankind that Lord Vishnu was our only savior? Why was there the contradiction, is what I was unable to grasp.

To get this answer I spent much time contemplating in frustration and rejecting answers knowing there had to be something more that he was trying to say that I was perhaps overlooking or not being able to interpret due to lack of understanding. It was while meditating that I got the answer to what I was seeking from a voice as if from heaven. It was not as if someone was speaking to me, but as if I was overhearing a discussion between two people. One who was being spoken to was referred to as Nikhil and the one speaking was Yama the lord of death, and such was the discussion that followed.

"My dear Nikhil, if one were to comprehend the Gayatri, it speaks about creation of the three worlds from a source where there was an explosion of the glorious light, defined as *Bhargo* in the Gayatri. The first manifestation was symbolically called Vishnu. This manifestation (Vishnu) has many attributes such as being full, the knower of all, knowing whom nothing more needs to be known, pure, blissful, the one with divine wisdom, all-powerful, full of strength, wealth and dispassion, all-pervading, eternal, infinite, he in me and I in him.

"Now introspect on the last sentence: he is in me and I in him. This gives the first hint of maya, the dream world. Everything that was created was in thought, dreams within dreams, the creation of the three worlds, one within the other. That's why Man also dreams because of that quality of the Creator. Remember, when I told you that through Vishnu was created Brahma and then the casual worlds and so on and so forth. All this is nothing but a dream within a dream.

"Now the question arises that what was the source of the creation of Vishnu, to which the answer is defined in the Gayatri as "*Tat*," meaning from that which all was created. That, Nikhil, is the formless aspect of Vishnu, the dark energy (Shakti) about which I have spoken to you before, the one without form, the ultimate truth called Brahman to which it is ascribed in the scriptures as Neti Neti: Not this, Not that, since it is beyond description."

"So, my lord," continued the gentleman referred to as Nikhil, "does this also means that Vishnu is a manifestation and, therefore, also subject to destruction?"

"Yes," replied Yama, "the death of Brahma is the awakening of Vishnu in his formless state. Now understand that the cause of creation was a reflection of all the qualities of the formless. However, with ignorance one forgot the purpose of his existence as did the gods because of false ego, thereby coming under the purview of karma. The reason I told you to educate mankind not to escape but to take bliss in the gift of life was because that was the cause for the formless Creator's creation . . . ."

Every doubt in my mind started to dissipate as I slowly, steadily but surely started comprehending and now realized why despite being a preacher of the Advaita Vedanta, Adi Sankaracharya stressed on the importance of falling at the feet of Vishnu as he was our only savior and conclusively came to the conclusion that I am about to tell.

In the beginning there was Brahman, the one without description since it is beyond comprehension, defined as Neti Neti in the ancient scriptures. One can also refer to Brahman as the formless aspect of Kali. In this cycle of creation and destruction there are two extremes of everything, like night and day, black and white and can be related with the architecture of the Yin and the Yang.

This formless aspect constitutes the mind, that is always present as the supreme soul. After a designated time the formless aspect starts to define itself and with its intellect creates the first manifestation which is "sound." This is followed by the vibrations of sound and the creation of a blueprint of its characteristics giving it the form of Goddess Kali.

The birth of Kali is the second manifestation of the supreme soul with its attributes even before the creation of light. It is for this reason that Goddess Kali is considered as the mother of creation. As spoken of in the scriptures, "Everything emerges from darkness and eventually dissolves into darkness." It is through this goddess that we are all created and it is into her that we will all eventually dissolve. With the birth of Kali now starts the creation of the opposite aspect of the supreme soul. The third manifestation is again of sound but, in a different frequency (Shiva), just after which the majestic and magnificent glorious light explodes creating the fourth manifestation, the birth of Vishnu. And through Vishnu, Brahma was born and so on and so forth.

Now despite the fact that Adi Sankaracharya said that Brahman was the ultimate truth, he was also hinting at the fact that as long as Lord Vishnu was not dissolved into his formless aspect we would be in a manifested stage, and so the only freedom that we could get was to merge and be one with Vishnu. To merge and be one with Brahman would be an eventuality that we are all destined to but, till then we must realize that the cause of creation was a reflection of all the qualities of the formless. However, with ignorance one forgot the purpose of his existence as did the gods because of false ego, thereby coming under the purview of karma. It is this journey that we must realize and undertake.

My mind was at peace. And quietly I sat down to meditate.

Over the next few days I started to go into bouts of meditation. I started to feel a strange kind of sensation at the bottom of my spine. I used to feel them before but this time it was different. It was like an electric current darting right across my spine and bursting like a small explosion at the top of my head. I would now regularly go into a state of Savikalpa Samadhi.

Over the next few months my meditation sessions got longer and I stated to get visions of the astral and casual worlds. I got all the answers that I had ever sought and for the first time experienced Nirvikalpa Samadhi.

I knew my past life and had a clear vision of so many of them. I saw myself as Swami Nachiketa, Nikhil and so many other names. I met many people I knew from the past. My friends, colleagues, relatives and so many saints who I believed to have been dead in the physical plane were present in the astral planets. It was a different world. How small my existence felt in the physical world as if being in a silly dream and not realizing that it was only a dream. I met my previous gurus and those who were guiding me and regained my knowledge from my past. I could continue staying here but chose to go back to the physical plane and analyze everything. I could always come back anytime I wanted to. The reason I chose to go back was because of what I recollected had been advised to me by lord Yama the lord of death in my transition from the previous to my current birth. That piece of information was vital and I realized that many in the high astral planets were also deprived of that knowledge.

As I slowly opened my eyes to my current physical form the room I was meditating in had a strange smell to it. There was nobody staying in the temple as I had locked it from outside and entered from a secret passage so as to give the impression that no one was in the temple. I switched on my mobile and looking at the date I realized that it was almost 15 days since I had been in the state of Nirvikalpa Samadhi although it felt only like a few hours or so, the reason being that the time zones are different as one travels into higher evolved astral planets.

My mind had expanded to a great degree and the body felt small. After cleaning up the temple I sat down to comprehend my journey with Yama the lord of death. I recollected the discussion in this regard.

"Once Man has been able to perceive what I have told you and the relevance of the philosophy of Gayatri, slowly his outlook toward life will start to change. Many get emotional at this stage, but remember, emotions have to get rejected. Many get passionate at this stage, and that too will have to be rejected, as these feelings will only deviate you from the correct path. Such emotions, Nikhil, may elevate you to higher astral worlds but not as a free soul. Once this fact is established one tends to start getting detached: that too will have to be rejected. With such introspection leading one's life the soul will start to comprehend its true nature as tools one may use what I have mentioned as this is the age of Kali, and comprehension alone may not suffice. As the days pass the lotus in you will start blooming or you may call it the rise of the symbolic snake coiled and asleep at the bottom of your spine. On the full blossoming of the 1,000-petalled lotus the bliss of which must also be rejected, on that day, Nikhil, tell mankind there will be a man standing in all his splendor, *The Free Soul*, The Greatest of the Greatest, Mightier that the Mightiest, Lord of the Lords, Lord Vishnu himself . . . ."

It was obvious to me now that Nirvikalpa Samadhi was not the end of the journey but there was more beyond. In Nirvikalpa Samadhi one gets transported to the high astral planets in which if he so chooses he can remain there and discard his physical body. Many great souls had achieved this. But to take the bliss of the astral world or choose to live a life in the physical form to help mankind was also a desire irrespective of how nice and holy it may sound, and if there is desire it bears the fruits of karma, if not in the physical then in the astral, if not in the astral then in the casual.

Here, it is most important to understand that being in human flesh reaching Nirvikalpa Samadhi is the highest goal that our physical body can endure. Here, one can use his free will to choose to stay in high astral planets or stay in the physical plane to serve mankind or any purpose that he may feel apt. If one has achieved the state of Nirvikalpa the karma of the physical world will have no effect on that person and one may do as he pleases.

I got into deeper meditation and once again reaching the stage of Nirvikalpa Samadhi I tried to force myself out of the astral planet finding myself on the border between the astral and casual worlds. It was imperative now that I discard my body in the physical plane. It mattered no more. In this stage there is only the mind and one becomes and has the attributes Brahma has (as in Brahma of the Holy Trinity and not Brahman that of the supreme soul).

Having reached this stage it is only the mind creating what it may please. Despite being here I did realize that there had to be still something beyond since my mind was in a mode of creating, stemming surely from the roots of desire hidden somewhere deep.

On this plane it is to be like the gods. One may manifest oneself in any form. Universes and worlds can be created in a flash. There are different levels of evolution in the casual world. One can evolve to higher levels or one may also come down to astral worlds.

I took bliss in the moment but knew this was not the final answer. I knew that much more effort would be required and rejected the freedom that came with this stage of my soul's evolution.

CHAPTER TWELVE

THE FINAL FRONTIER

The Free Soul

The time had come. As I waited to discard my casual existence and enter the final truth, I felt the bliss of nothingness as my mind was darting into the final awakening.

The glorious light shone with all its brightness, like nothing ever seen before, nothing that could possibly have been imagined. I was the light that emerged out of the darkness. The entire existence in me as I in them.

I am the truth,
I am the reality,
I am the universe,
I am the light,
I am the darkness,
I am Brahma,
I am Vishnu,
I am Shiva,
I am Christ,
I am Buddha,
I am the Vedas,
I am the Upanishads,
I am the Gayatri,
The entire cosmic play is the blueprint of my thought.

I am everywhere,
I am the final truth,
I am the only truth,
I am light when I am asleep,
I am dark when I am awake.
Everything and Nothingness are both my qualities, both sides of the same coin revolving in the cosmic play of night and day.
I am the Free Soul.
Come to me as I wait to welcome you. Look not ahead but within.
Wake up now, the time has come.
Feel me within you: I have always been there.
Why do you reject me with your veil of ignorance?
Why do you seek me for worldly pleasures when you are me and everything is already yours?
To be a free soul is your right, but why have you forgotten your free will?
Throw away your sadness. Spit it out like a bitter seed.
Cry over nothing; the world was created for joy.
Use my power within you to battle the illusion of life.
Know that your soul is no different from mine.
Feel me in your every breath.
Embrace me as your friend and I shall guide you to the right path.
I have no religion.
I have no caste.
Like a light I shine in each one's heart.
I am waiting for you,
Wake up now, my child, the time has come.
Do not grieve for the dead,
Do not grieve for those alive,
Life and death are only a transition in your journey to come to me,
Why do you waste it in vain?
I have come to you once again in this age and time
To hold your hands.
Feel me next to you as you read these lines.
Wake up now, my child, the time has come.
Seek not my flesh for blessings but my words for the journey I wish each one to take.
The body is just a tool like a vehicle used for transportation.
I shall be watching all and reveal myself to those who seek me and when you find me we shall be one.

There is no End because there never was a beginning.

EPILOGUE

This novel is work of fiction influenced by the ancient scriptures of Hindu philosophy. Don't believe a word of what has been said. This is what I want you to do. If you can do that, it is good.

Now you have started your journey.
Reject:
Introspect:
Contemplate:
Till the time that you find the true nature of your soul.
In the meantime let us enjoy this game of "Hide and Seek."
I will keep providing you with hints.
You may refer to me as "The Swami."